# GOING FINISH

## MANDY MARONEY

ISBNs:

978-1-7643012-0-6 (paperback)

978-1-7643012-1-3 (ebook)

Editing and interior typesetting by Claire McGregor, Kookaburra Hill Publishing Services

Cover design by Hamish Payne

***Going finish***, an anglicised version of the pidgin *go pinis*, means final farewell and came to refer to the mass exodus of expats leaving Papua New Guinea around the time of its Independence in 1975.

*To my parents, Paul and Marylou, for giving me and my brother, Guy, an unforgettable childhood in Papua New Guinea.*

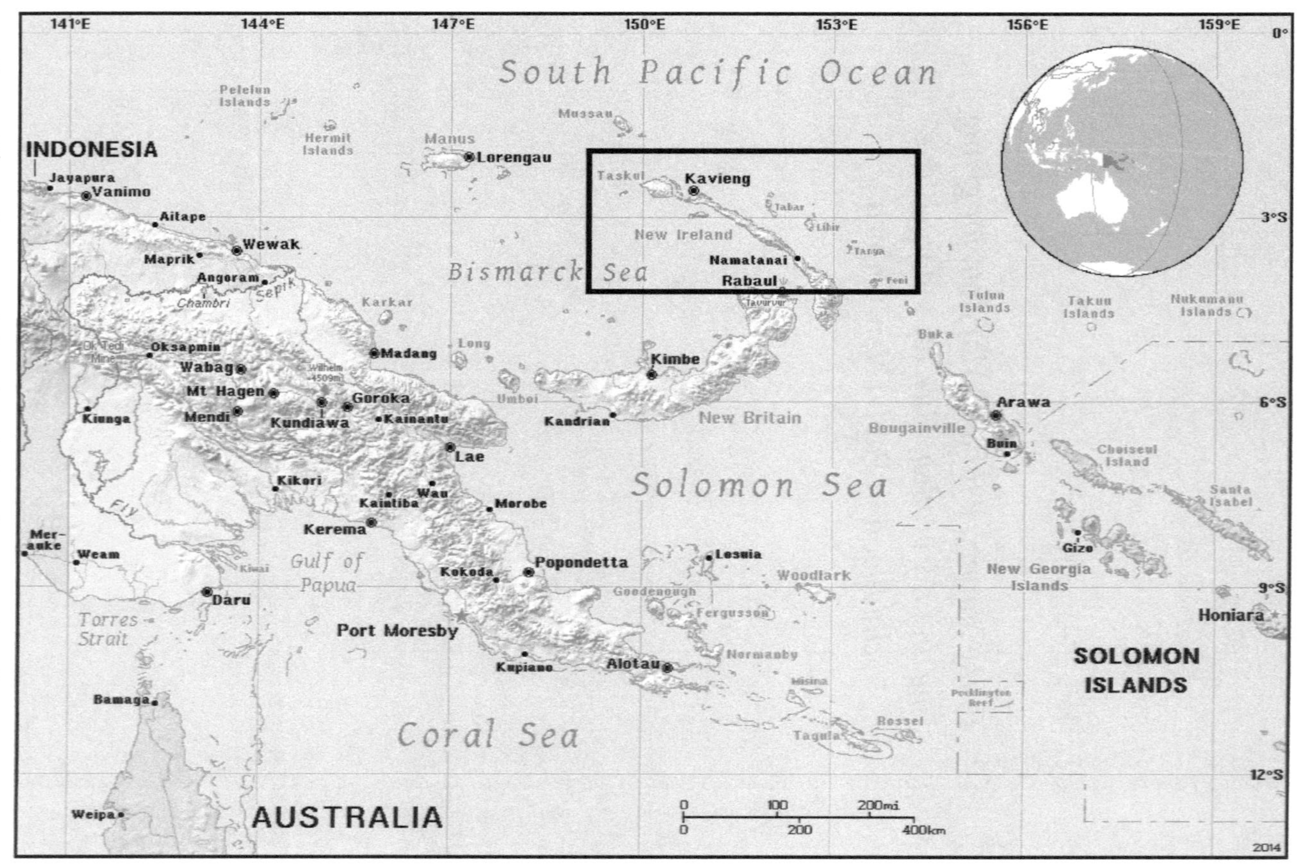


*Source: The author gratefully acknowledges the generosity of Ian Mackey, mapmaker, who makes his excellent maps freely available.*

# Prologue

## August–September 1985

I nearly didn't check the letterbox that afternoon. My last delivery should have taken five minutes but Miss Beckett got me talking about canna lilies. We both loved those proud plants so I had lingered and the sun was sinking as I steered the truck back between our gate posts. Habit alone made me pull up, roll down the window and drop my hand to the letterbox.

The envelope I pulled out felt substantial. I could just make out a bird of paradise crest and the words *Independen Stet Bilong Papua Niugini.* I sat in the half-light wondering what it could mean. Almost twelve years had passed since my family had left PNG, had *gone finish*, as they used to say, but it felt like a lifetime. We hadn't so much left as fled, and

I'd squashed down the memories. Until now.

Once inside, I sat on a kitchen stool and opened the letter. It announced that William Cleary had been awarded the highest honour the country could bestow in recognition of his sacrifice. Family members were invited to attend a ceremony on September 16th, 1985, in conjunction with the celebration of the country's tenth anniversary of independence. It was signed 'The Honourable Member for New Ireland Province' and scrawled in red biro below was the message 'Can't wait to see you again, hey!' That schoolboy exclamation mark made my stomach drop like an air pocket.

I phoned my mother.

'Hel-l-o-o.'

'Mum, it's me, Billie. Did you get it?'

'I received a letter, if that's what you're referring to?'

'What do you think?'

There was a long pause.

'I can't believe the nerve of that boy.'

'He's hardly a boy. He must be at least thirty.'

'Well, the nerve of that man, then.'

'Mum, try not to get worked up.'

Silence echoed down the line.

'Mum?'

A muffled sound like a sob.

'Are you okay, Mum?'

'It's hard to believe it can still get to me, after all these years.'

'Twelve years isn't that long.'

'Why is he raking it all up again? I just don't know what Lionel's going to make of it.'

My shoulders tensed. 'It's got nothing to do with Lionel.'

My mother had met Lionel the year after we'd left PNG, at a club for returned expatriates on the North Shore. He'd been a District Commissioner, like Dad, but a more refined version. My sisters and I all agreed he was perfect for Mum. Upper crust, just like her, in a way Dad had never been.

Lionel had given my mother a new life and we were grateful for that. It wasn't my stepfather I resented, it was my mother. The way she bent over backwards to avoid the slightest mention of my father. As though it would be easier for everyone if he'd never existed.

'It would put poor Lionel in a very awkward position if I were to accept this invitation.'

'I think you underestimate him.'

There was a theatrical pause. 'Well, anyway, I'm not going.'

Another long pause. 'The man's obviously trying to buy our silence with his ridiculous medal.'

I struggled to keep my voice steady. 'Why can't it just be what it claims to be, an award to honour Dad?'

'Because nothing that man does is straightforward. He's just like his father. Couldn't lie straight in bed.'

'Mum, you know he wasn't involved, don't you? In what happened to Dad.'

'Tell yourself that if it makes you feel better, Billie.'

Her words stung. Suddenly I was sixteen again, not knowing which way was up, who could be trusted and who couldn't.

I slammed down the phone and was immediately sorry. I didn't just feel like a sixteen year old, I was acting like one. The damned letter had me unhinged.

Headlights swept the driveway, catching a flash of colour. My beloved cannas. They had been the first thing I'd planted here. Whenever their rooster comb heads fluttered, I caught the bittersweet memory of blinding sunlight and the foreshadowing of loss.

The front door banged and he was standing in the hallway. He looked so happy I couldn't bear to spoil things just yet.

It wasn't until we'd finished dinner that I pushed the letter across the table. 'You'll never guess who I heard from today?'

He glanced over its contents. 'Honourable Member, hey?'

His chuckle reminded me of Dad.

'I know.' I sniggered.

'Funny, though, him getting back in touch after all this time.'

My cheeks burnt. 'He's not getting in touch with *me*. It's addressed to *all* of us.'

'What does your mother think?'

'Since when do you care what my mother thinks?'

'So, she doesn't trust him either?'

'Why can't people believe he's just doing the right thing?'

'People? Since when have I been "people"?'

'I'm sorry.' I reached for his hand. 'I guess it's unnerved me, hearing from him again. Out of the blue …'

He squeezed back. 'You don't have to go, you know.'

'Do you really think I want to leave you to go back there, even if it's just for a few days?'

'So, don't.'

'It's a chance to find out the truth. You know I can't pass that up.'

'You really think he's going to tell you the truth?'

'I'll know if he doesn't.'

He shook his head. 'He always knew how to play you, Billie.'

'Ouch.' I grabbed up the plates and headed for the kitchen, afraid tears might give me away.

He came up from behind as I stood at the sink and wrapped his arms around me. 'Let me come with you then.'

It was tempting. From the moment he'd walked back into my life, he was the one who looked out for me. But my gut told me I had to do this alone.

I leant back into him. 'I think I need to go by myself.'

'You're sure?'

'As sure as I'll ever be. You'll just have to trust me on that one.'

He held me tighter and I closed my eyes. Some nights I still returned to those faraway islands in my dreams, and they were fevered dreams of heat, skin and danger. Truth was, I didn't really trust myself.

Brisbane Airport looked tired and smaller than I remembered. My sister Rosie emerged from the crowd in a hot-pink shimmer and heads turned. She still had a lovely face but her fluorescent lipstick was a touch too bright. She lived on the Gold Coast and the brighter the better on Cavill Avenue.

I was surprised she was coming with us; her second husband was a shocking womaniser, and I didn't think she'd risk leaving him to his own devices for even a day. But she'd never been one to miss a party. She pulled me into a tight hug of Chanel No. 5 and stale wine.

'Hi, sis. How's that sweet boyfriend of yours?'

'Sweet as ever.'

Rosie winked. 'But you couldn't resist your old squeeze, could you?'

'He's not my old squeeze.'

'What do you think he wants then?'

'Maybe he just wants to make amends? Now he can?'

'Smacks of a guilty conscience, if you ask me.'

'That's what Mum said, but I thought *you'd* understand …'

'Are you two at it already?' Susan strode towards us grinning, but she looked tired and older than her thirty-two years. She dressed old too, just like Mum, in a jacket that was going to be way too hot for Port Moresby.

After we hugged, Rosie pointed across the plaza. 'The bar's open, girls. Let's go toast the old man.'

'What were you two arguing about?' Susan asked, as we settled around a table.

'Rosie thinks this medal's the sign of a guilty conscience.'

'You said yourself he wants to make amends. Amends for what exactly?' Rosie raised her eyebrows.

I turned to Susan. 'What do you think?'

'I'm not sure what I think. That's why I'm here.'

The waiter filled our glasses with a flourish.

'What does that boyfriend of yours make of it, Billie?' Susan asked.

'I guess he thinks it's a bit strange, coming out of the blue like that.'

'Bet he's jealous.' Rosie grinned.

'Why would he be?'

'Oh, come on, Billie, you're jumping out of your skin.'

'I'm … just on edge, that's all.'

Susan patted my hand. 'Poor kid.'

'Nothing this stuff won't fix.' Rosie clinked her glass against mine.

I gulped the wine, but I knew she was wrong. An uneasiness had lodged in my chest the moment I'd set eyes on that letter and no amount of alcohol was going to melt it.

We sat in awkward silence until Rosie asked if either of us had spoken to Mum and we were back in familiar territory, swapping jokes about my mother's snobbery and Lionel's cravat collection.

My uneasiness lingered as we sat in a row on the plane waiting for take-off. It pushed down on my chest as we raced along the runway, and when we were jerked into the air and the earth fell away, it felt like I was hurtling back to an inescapable fate.

# Chapter I

## Going home, December 1973

Our last trip to that place had started like all the others. Woken by torchlight, Rosie and I dressed in the dark to catch the early bus up to Brisbane. It was thrilling being the only ones awake in the dormitory, like prisoners about to break out.

We had a long day ahead of us. The terminals and the planes would get smaller until we finally pulled up on the tarmac in Kavieng, New Ireland, as the sun was about to dip below the horizon.

Everything had gone to plan on the bus and in Brisbane Airport, and now the jet was levelling off high above the city sprawl. As soon as the seatbelt sign pinged off, Rosie nudged me towards the toilets. I pushed into one of the tiny cubicles and struggled out of the straitjacket of my blazer. Perching on the closed toilet seat, I yanked off my ugly school shoes and sweaty pantyhose and wriggled my toes around a bit before slipping on my sandals.

Shedding our school uniforms was one of the rituals of going home that we'd looked forward to for the last three months. We knew my mother wouldn't approve but we gambled on the fact that she'd be so pleased to see us after a school term away that she wouldn't punish us. It was the season of goodwill after all, and hopefully even my mother would be full of it.

Rosie came back several minutes after me in an impossibly pink tank top. Mum would hate it but she'd probably hate my denim shorts more. I could hear her already, saying something like, 'I wish you'd try to be more feminine, Billie.'

After she'd settled back into her seat, Rosie looked me up and down and offered a pot of lip-gloss. 'You're quite pretty, Billie, in a subtle way. You just need a bit of help. After all, you never know who you might meet on the way home.'

It was easier if I didn't try to compete with my sister. Subtlety had no chance against her blonde curls and her belly button winking below the pink top. Boys were Rosie's thing, and she was welcome to them.

First stop was Port Moresby Airport. The heat was solid and we struggled against it down the scorching metal stairs, bags bulging with our discarded school clothes and shoes. As we crossed the tarmac, another wave of heat shimmered up to meet us.

With the heat came the smells. Sweaty bodies, hair oil, tobacco, overripe fruit and the elusive but ever-present citrus mix of betel nut and lime all wafted over from groups of local people sitting or leaning against fences around the terminal. We picked our way around bright orange puddles of betel nut juice.

We found relief from the burning sun under the wide roof of the terminal. Everything was open to let breezes waft through, and the ceiling fans constantly clicked.

The first sign of change during our term away was right there at the check-in desk. Air Niugini, the new national airline, had been operating for just a couple of months, but already the desk was manned by a Papuan. He was dressed exactly as his white counterpart would have been, in short-sleeved shirt, shorts and long socks, but he didn't look comfortable. I tried to give him an encouraging smile but his eyes scurried away. He called me 'Missus', although he must have been at least twice my age.

To fill in time until the boarding call, I walked across

to the kiosk to buy a couple of cold Fantas, a magazine for Rosie and a copy of the *Post Courier* for me. We never got to see a newspaper at boarding school, and there was something comforting about the *Post Courier*, with its golfing results, Fred Bassett cartoons and Pidgin ads for Velvet soap and bully beef. It was the kind of paper in which you might read about someone you actually knew.

I noticed that quite a few of the young local men I passed were wearing t-shirts with political slogans. The Pangu Pati's bird of paradise, with its orange tail feathers, seemed to have replaced South Pacific beer as the favourite logo.

The sweaty man behind the kiosk counter was wearing a yellowing singlet, and I tried not to look at the hair sticking out from his armpits in ginger clumps.

He gestured towards the paper I'd picked up. 'It's all over now, girlie. The lunatics have taken over the asylum.'

The front-page headline read: 'What Self-Government Means for PNG'.

'We'll all be out on our arses soon.' He leant forward and dropped his voice. 'Bloody Labor Party's handing it to the coons on a platter. Everything *we've* worked for.'

I was shocked into silence by that ugly word. It was only as I was relating the conversation to Rosie that the anger rose in my throat. 'That "we" really gets me. Why do the bigots always assume you feel the same way just because you're white?'

'Get used to it, we're back in the sticks now. Pass the *Cleo*, would you?'

Soon we were shuffling back into the glare. On the tarmac sat a Fokker Friendship, sporting the familiar bird of paradise logo on its tail. A much smaller plane than the last, it only carried about fifty passengers.

We hit turbulence as we flew north across the Owen Stanley Range and the bulkhead shook like it was made of flimsy plastic. I gripped the seat arms.

'Don't worry, my dear,' said the lady sitting across the aisle.

The big gold cross around her neck marked her as a missionary. She wore pantyhose with her sandals, and I felt a jolt of static electricity as she leant over to pat my hand.

'The Lord isn't ready to take us yet, dear. He's just giving us a bit of fun.' She grinned at me as though we were on a scary ride at a show.

My anticipation grew as each landing brought us closer to home. Rabaul was the last stop before Kavieng and the approach over its emerald harbour was spectacular. Six volcanoes circled the town, and during the 1937 eruption two more jagged peaks had broken through its waters. They stuck out still – a stark reminder that all this beauty could be wrenched apart one day by a destructive force lurking beneath its surface.

The final descent took us right over one of the craters, so close I could see grass running down into its dark core. Then we were flying low over the glassy waters towards the airstrip, which reached into the harbour on a narrow finger of land. It felt as though we might topple off the runway into the sea. I held my breath as we thumped down onto the asphalt.

The plane taxied to a halt and the noise of the engines fell away to an ear-ringing silence. An awkwardly long pause followed. Our fellow passengers started to fidget and look around for some hint of what was causing the delay, and still the minutes ticked away. I started to feel anxious. The connecting flight to Kavieng had to leave in plenty of time before the sun began to sink in the sky, and my watch read quarter to five.

The public address system crackled, and the gentle voice of our air hostess murmured something about passengers going on to Kavieng. Rosie and I looked at each other. The rest of the passengers had begun shuffling down the aisle, so we followed them.

Rosie tugged on the sleeve of the airport worker at the bottom of the stairs.

'What did she say about Kavieng?'

'Pilot emi no happy. Onepela engine i-bugger up.'

I wanted to cry.

'No worry, missus.' The man grinned with the legendary Tolai charm. 'Twin Otter, emi kisim you i-go long Kavieng.' He gestured across the tarmac to a smaller, pointy-nosed plane, its two engines sitting high up on its wings.

The crew took us straight over to the waiting plane. The air inside was heavy with sweat and frustration. I shuffled along the aisle, trying not to bump the passengers on either side with my bag. Rosie and I were at the tail end of the line of transferring passengers, so there were only a couple of seats left when we got up to the air hostess. She beckoned me into a seat next to a boy sitting by the window.

He had a grown-up look about him; he was wearing a rugby jersey and shorts, and his skin was a glossy brown.

I placed my hand on the armrest to steady myself and my skin looked so pale next to his. He touched one of my fingers and I felt a jolt, but this time it wasn't static electricity.

He gestured in Rosie's direction. 'If you two are together, I can move?'

'It's okay … I'm happy here.' Rosie winked at me as she slid into the seat in front.

The boy leant towards me as I settled back. If he had

noticed my stunning sister, he didn't show it. I was glad I'd changed out of my uniform and smeared on a bit of Rosie's lip-gloss.

'I'm Errol,' he said.

I understood the reason for Rosie's wink as I took a better look. He was closer to beautiful than any boy I'd ever seen. His almond eyes had a languid half-closed look, as though weighed down by their thick black lashes. His features were very fine, except his lips, which were almost too full. Almost, but not quite.

'Are you from Kavieng?' I asked.

'Nuh, little place down the road called Keriva. My mum runs the trade store.'

'What were you doing in Rabaul?'

'I stopped over to visit one of my aunties. On the way back from uni in Brisbane.'

'Uni? Wow. What are you studying?'

'Politics. Don't know if I'll bother going back next year though. Might learn more here.' He looked at me expectantly. 'I've seen you around – you're one of the DC's daughters, aren't you?'

I nodded.

'Daddy's a District Commissioner – very posh.' His voice coaxed me along gently. He smiled a lazy smile, and I could see the tip of his tongue, pink behind his white teeth. When he gazed at me I felt it in the pit of my stomach, and I didn't want him to stop.

# Chapter 2

## Homecoming

The next thirty minutes slipped away too quickly. Errol talked about his mother and the aunt he'd been visiting in Rabaul, and I watched him, entranced. He was so confident, so easy in his own skin, so different from any boy I'd ever met.

Every so often, he reached across to touch my hand or brush my arm and everything else went out of my head. I was overwhelmed by the thought that we would soon be landing and I would have no more reason to be with him.

We'd been flying over the coconut plantations that ran the length of New Ireland for a while, and now I could see water through the windows on both sides of the plane. My heart jolted as I saw the familiar sight of Kavieng Harbour, its tiny islands strung together like a jade bracelet against the aqua velvet of the sea. The plane began to circle back towards the airstrip.

I loved the moment, as the plane was coming down, when the scene changed from looking like lines on a map to real roads and real cars and real people waiting next to the strip. I couldn't help leaning across to try to make out the figures of my parents, and Errol turned towards me, so his lips were almost touching my neck. I could feel his breath on my skin.

'Don't s'pose you get down to Keriva very often? Never mind – I'm up in town quite a bit. I drive a VW Fastback. Keep an eye out for it.'

I could sense Errol behind me as we shuffled down the aisle, but when I turned to say goodbye at the cyclone-wire gate, he wasn't there anymore.

My father stood a whole head above the rest of the waiting crowd. He still looked like a skinny kid. Knuckle-bound hands hung heavy at the end of his weathered forearms. He wasn't wearing a hat, but he had the bushman's way of hooding his eyes against the glare, so he looked as though he didn't need one.

When I was younger, Dad had screened films at the high school, and when he'd shown one of Clarke Gable's set in Africa, I couldn't figure out how Dad got to be up on the screen and next to me at the same time. The actor up there had Dad's khakis, his hooded eyes, even the gruff manner that made everyone around him feel easier. But he didn't have Dad's eyes. When my father smiled and flashed his sea-green eyes, you felt like the luckiest person in the world.

Rosie broke into a jog as we passed the gate. I let her push through to hug Mum, so I was the first to get to Dad. As those bony hands held each side of my head and he bent to place a kiss on my hair, I knew I was home. Everything I loved about the place was wrapped up with my father.

On the drive home, I mentioned the *Post Courier* article.

'Is self-government the same as independence?' I asked.

'It's a stepping stone,' Dad said. 'We keep control of the big things, like defence and the courts, until independence. Doesn't seem like it's going to be a long wait.'

I told him about the man at the kiosk.

'I don't like his language,' Dad said, 'but I've got to agree with his sentiment.'

I was shocked. 'But isn't self-government a good thing? It is their country, after all.'

'They're not ready, kid. Some of them will never be ready.'

It was the first time I'd ever heard my father say anything bad about PNG. And there was a mean note in his voice I didn't like.

On our first morning home, my mother had Tahl set the breakfast table with her special china and decorate each place with a hibiscus flower. Mum grew up in a house where breakfast was delivered on a tray and laundry disappeared down a chute, and she couldn't resist treating Tahl and his wife like old family retainers. They'd been with my parents for more than twenty years, so in a way they were.

Tahl was a Highlander, small and compact, built for climbing mountain passes and walking all day. My mother had trained him to keep a 'straight face' like an English butler, but we girls loved to coax a smile out of him as he stood at the end of the table.

Suriwan came from very different stock. She was taller than her husband, with sturdy legs and an expressive face across which emotion passed easily. She let out a squeal when she saw us and pinched Rosie's cheeks with delight. She'd carried each of us as babies in a *lap-lap* next to her body, and that physical bond remained. Only my mother's presence stopped the three of us from throwing our arms around each other.

'I do miss having you girls around,' Mum said, as we squeezed lemon juice over our pawpaw. 'The good china is wasted on your father. And Susan will be here next week.'

My eldest sister, Susan, had started nursing in Sydney two years earlier. She had settled in so well down south it was easy to forget she'd ever lived in PNG. She'd never liked getting dirty and I didn't remember her going barefoot, even at the beach. It was like she'd been born a grown-up.

After breakfast, I escaped into the back garden. This had always been my special place. Vines had plaited themselves around fallen trees and the bush hovered, waiting to move back in. I closed my eyes and breathed in the overripe air. In the wet season the moisture built through the day until the rain set it free about three o'clock, and that fresh smell was one of the things I'd missed. I lay back against the soft undergrowth and breathed in freedom.

It wasn't long before Mum called me 'to run some errands'. She liked to keep us busy doing the kind of things she thought young ladies should do. We went down to Burns Philp, the general store, and walked the aisles picking up a handful of provisions. Mum's real reason for the outing was to show us off and bask in the usual comments about what beautiful girls we were growing into. Everyone looked at Rosie when they said this.

Then Mum took us to the library to choose some 'holiday reading'. She shook her head at the copy of *The Catcher in the Rye* I picked up and collected a pile of Agatha Christies she thought more suitable. Rosie borrowed a couple of Mills & Boons to keep my mother happy, but I knew she had a copy of *Mandingo*, the latest risqué book going around school, hidden under her pillow. Mum would have had a fit if she'd seen the half-naked black slave on the cover.

I had a restless feeling all day that grew as the shadows lengthened. Everything looked the same, but it felt different. Ever since the plane had landed yesterday and we'd gone our separate ways, all I could think of was Errol.

When I came into the kitchen next morning, Dad was whistling over a spluttering frying pan.

'Got to fatten you girls up after that crook boarding school tucker. You'll need a good feed today – I'm taking you waterskiing.'

I felt my chest lift with excitement, but Rosie looked bored.

'Bags being the lookout,' she said.

Dad and I grinned at each other. Rosie always spent as much time as she could in the boat, working on her tan.

Rosie's bikini was crimson, tied at the side and very brief.

'Where on earth did you get that?' Mum asked.

Rosie shot me a sly grin and I remembered she'd borrowed my spare sports tunic all last term. She must have bought the bikini with the money Mum had sent her for a new tunic. I looked down at my faded gingham two-piece and had a flash of inspiration. I'd make my own, using Rosie's bikini as a pattern. There were always useful scraps of material in Mum's sewing box. I wouldn't need much.

We loaded the dinted Esky into the station wagon and drove down to the harbour. The view of the sea was framed by huge shade trees and the contrast made the water sparkle brighter and bluer than seemed possible.

Dad parked next to where the government speedboats were moored. We waded out to the nearest one in old sandshoes. In this part of the harbour the sea floor was peppered with sea urchins, whose spines broke off in unprotected feet. The only way to get rid of them was to pound them into a pulp while they were still in your foot – a fate horrible enough to ensure that we all wore our Dunlops into the water.

Once we were all on board, Dad headed straight for the pair of islands in the middle of Kavieng Harbour, called Nusa and Nusa Lik, or little Nusa. The twin islands were perfect in their simplicity. Each was small enough to walk around and a shallow channel ran between them. You could wade from one to the other or lie on your stomach in the middle. We always picnicked on the larger island, Nusa, where a clearing shaded by palms sprawled next to the beach.

Mum sat gingerly in the middle of the boat, clutching her seat and the paisley scarf around her head. She was nervous about boating, as she was about many of the things we loved. Dad dropped her straight out to the island so she could prepare the picnic at leisure.

'Right,' he shouted as he turned the boat back out into open water, as if to say *Now we'll have some fun.* He revved the engine so hard it screamed, and he grinned at us like a naughty child.

The rest of the morning passed in a blur of spray. I loved the feeling of sliding across the top of the water on skis, eyes screwed up against the wind, and the wake spattering against my legs. It seemed only a few minutes had passed before Dad made his windup signal and pulled me into the boat to head in for lunch.

Back on the island, Mum stood above a fly-proof net, which she removed with a flourish, like a second-rate magician, to reveal the picnic spread underneath. The tartan rug was covered with plates of what Dad called 'horses' doovers' to tease Mum; asparagus wrapped in white bread and toothpicks strung with tinned pineapple, cheese cubes and cabana. There were delicious fresh pineapples at the local market, but Mum didn't trust anything that didn't come in a tin.

As soon as I'd stuffed a few down, I headed back to the water.

'You should wait at least half an hour before you go in,' my mother called across the sand. I quickly submerged as though I hadn't heard her. I'd daydreamed about lying in that channel between the two islands for a whole school term and no threat of cramp was going to keep me out of there.

One wet afternoon last term, as we lay on the gym floor, the sports teacher had taught us relaxation. 'Imagine your favourite place,' she shouted above the din of rain on the tin roof, and I was back in that channel, floating in water as warm as blood, my belly scraping the sand.

When my mother finally came in for a swim, she lowered herself as though she were on a conveyer belt. Her hairdo, lipstick and sunglasses all remained untouched as she slowly submerged to the neck. I looked at her, and then at Rosie – sunbaking with leftover cucumber slices on her eyes – and wondered again how we could all be related.

'Come for a walk with me, Billie?' Dad held out his hand and I jumped up.

The sun was beginning to sting my back, so I grabbed a t-shirt. Dad had on the faded blue terry-towelling hat he always wore out in the boat.

We didn't speak until we had walked around to the far side of the island. Waves were rolling in, erasing our footprints as we made them. The ocean stretched to the horizon.

'It looks like we're on the edge of the world,' I said.

'Oh, there are hundreds of islands out there. But they're flat so you don't see them until you're about to run aground.'

As if on cue, a canoe appeared a few hundred yards out from us. The two men in it waved and then continued reeling in their net.

'It's so good being out where the real people live,' Dad said. 'I wish those office johnnies in Moresby would come out here before they make any more decisions about this country's future.'

'What do you think will happen?'

'It's become a hot potato. Whitlam's been trying to get out of this country ever since he got into power. I spend most of my days now training my replacement, Nathan.'

'Is that bad?'

'Don't get me wrong – Nathan's a good bloke, keen as mustard, but he needs a couple of years to get up to scratch, and the jokers want me to hand over in six months.' He put his hand on my shoulder. 'I expect we'll soon be joining all the other expats *going finish*. This could well be our last Christmas here.'

I didn't know what to say. Dad loved the place as much as I did.

We walked the rest of the way around the island in silence. But the conversation kept going around in my head. This wasn't just politics – it was our home we were talking about.

# Chapter 3

## Lucille

Mum sought me out the next morning after breakfast. She'd forgotten it was Ladies Lunch day at the Golf Club. Could I ever forgive her? After waving her off, I sat on a fallen coconut tree in our back garden to enjoy the peace. A light breeze tickled my cheek.

A horn tooted, a short burst at first and then more persistently. I peered down through the knotted vines and saw a rusty maroon car parked on the harbour road. It was a VW Fastback.

I picked my way through the undergrowth as fast as I could, ignoring the sharp kunai grass slashing my legs.

Errol rolled down the window. 'Wondered if you'd like to go for a drive? Meet some people?'

'That'd be great. I'll just let my sister know …'

He raised his eyebrows, and I felt suddenly juvenile.

Back in the house, I slipped into my room and changed into my shortest shorts. I was on my way out when Rosie's voice startled me. 'Where are you sneaking off to, little sister?'

I blushed.

'You're going to meet that boy, aren't you?'

'What if I am?'

'Be careful, Billie. You know what they're like.'

'You don't know anything about him. Anyway, you can't talk. You're always sneaking off with the Warwick boys.'

'It's not *what* you do – it's *who* you do it with. Remember that, Billie.'

'*I* remember finding you and Stuart Warwick up against the back wall of the Golf Club last holidays. Mum wouldn't be so happy to throw you at those boys if she knew what you really got up to.'

We sized each other up for a moment and then she said quietly, 'I won't tell if you don't.'

'Deal.'

I hadn't thought through what I was doing until I'd already slammed the car door behind me. But as Errol revved the engine and the car took off with a jolt, I realised that driving off with a boy I hardly knew was exactly the kind of thing Rosie would do.

Errol smiled a knowing smile, as though he could read my mind. 'Don't worry, I'm just taking you to meet my favourite cousin, the one I stay with when I'm in town.'

I tried not to stare. His shorts and singlet didn't cover much of that gleaming skin, and I was acutely aware of his thighs splayed on the seat a few inches from my hand.

Five minutes down the coast road, we turned up a driveway and parked in front of a small fibro house at the top of the rise. A spindly frangipani tree stood out the front and the distinctive fragrance of its lemon-centred flowers wafted on the sea breeze.

'Lucille,' Errol called.

A tiny Chinese woman in a polka-dot sundress emerged, rubbing her hands together in delight. She ran towards us as fast as someone wearing three-inch heels could and threw her arms around Errol's neck.

'How lovely to see you again, darling.' She looked me over with friendly interest. 'Who have you brought this time?'

'I'm Billie.' I tried not to think about what she meant by *this time*.

'The DC's daughter?'

I nodded.

'Delighted,' she purred.

The three of us sat on a worn sofa on her verandah overlooking the harbour. The view from this little house was every bit as good as the one from our place. Lucille poured tea from a delicately patterned pot. Her legs were crossed like a perfect lady's, the foot of her top leg neatly tucked behind the other. The toenails peeping out from the white straps of her sandals were the same shade of baby pink as her inch-long fingernails. With her sleek fringe and rosebud lips, she was easily the most glamorous person I'd ever met.

She turned to Errol. 'So, how long are you staying this time?'

Errol flashed a wide smile. 'Now we've got self-government, I thought I might stick around. Make sure they hand it over fair and square.'

Lucille frowned. 'I don't want you getting into any trouble.'

She turned to me. 'This boy's special. For years, I looked after him for Uncle Cedric. The poor little fellow only stopped crying when I carried him around in my arms. I wasn't much more than a child myself, but I guess he became like a son to me.'

Errol pulled an embarrassed face, but I could tell he was touched.

'Why can't you just stay here with me?' she implored.

Errol crossed his arms. 'They need me.'

'Cedric never needed anyone but himself. And as for her ... well, she made her choice the day she let him take her child away.'

'She did it for *me*, to give me opportunities. It was the right thing to do.' He paused. 'But I was talking about my people. *They're* the ones who need me now.'

I sat there like a dummy, shocked that Lucille had criticised Errol's mother. I barely knew him, but from the look on his face it was clear his mother was off-limits.

'Baby, I'm just worried. Things are changing so fast. You might get involved in something.' She reached for his arm, but he jerked away.

'Things *need* to change, the faster, the better. And I *should* be involved. Otherwise, what was all that sacrifice for?'

There was a long silence as Lucille looked him up and down. 'Maybe you're more like him than you realise.'

Errol's chair clattered as he stood. 'We'd better go.' He raised his eyebrows at me and gestured towards the car.

I was stunned. Arguments were something that happened behind closed doors in my home. The emotions between Lucille and Errol had been so raw, but as she walked us back to the car, they acted like nothing had happened, as though this sort of thing was normal between them.

'Lovely to meet you, Billie.' Lucille said. 'By the way, do you ever go to Pearlie's boutique?'

I shook my head. I had no idea there was anything that could be called a boutique in Kavieng.

'Maybe I'll drop by sometime, take you shopping.'

Instead of taking me home, Errol drove around the headland to the ocean beach. We sat in the car and listened to the waves pounding on the rocks. I searched his face for clues about how he felt but he looked directly ahead, impassive as a wooden carving.

'You said Lucille was your *cousin*,' I said. 'I'm not quite sure I understand ...'

'Didn't you guess? With all that talk about "Uncle Cedric"?'

There was an awkward silence.

'You don't have to talk about it if you don't want to.' I looked at his hand on the seat between us, wanting to comfort him.

'I'm what they call a bastard.'

'Oh.'

'And that's not the worst of it. The most likely candidate's good old "Uncle Cedric". He looked at me expectantly.

'So?'

'Guess you haven't met him then. He's our local member of parliament but only because he buys votes.'

'Oh.'

'The type who'd sell his own grandmother if he thought it'd help him get on.'

'Does he really buy votes?'

'He hands out free bottles of beer before the elections, which amounts to the same thing. Anyway, he paid my school fees down south, and last year he gave me his old car. There's only one reason a prick like him would do something like that.'

I finally found the courage to reach across and take his hand. It felt warm and moist, and our skin stuck together as he gently pulled his hand back.

'It's okay,' he said. 'I just wanted to tell you before someone else did.'

I was gazing at him and thinking, *Of course he had a Chinese father – that was why his hair was jet black and dead straight.*

There was an awkward silence before he spoke again. 'I can't believe Lucille said that. About me being like him.'

'I'm sure she didn't mean it.'

He looked at me like I was stupid. 'She meant it all right. She's trying to scare me off politics. She wants me to live up here in town like a white man, forget the village.' He was fiddling with something on a chain around his neck as he spoke. 'She doesn't see that now I can really help my people.'

His eyes shone and I felt his passion. He was good at it. He sounded like he was giving a speech, his voice rising and falling and pausing after the important points. But I couldn't help hoping he'd stick around town a little longer. The last thing I wanted was for him to disappear down to his village.

# Chapter 4

## Chinatown

I didn't hear from Errol for the next few days, so I read my way through the Agatha Christies. I was on the last one when I heard Lucille's voice floating down our hall. I hurried towards the door with a nervous flutter in my stomach.

Lucille was immaculate in a white dress with matching sunhat. My mother, in her usual brown tones, was a moth next to a butterfly.

'Billie, there's someone here for you.' Mum's voice was raised unnecessarily as I approached.

'I'm Lucille Chan, Mrs Cleary.'

'Can I help you with something?'

'I've come to take Billie shopping. Would you believe she'd never even heard of Pearlie's boutique?'

My mother looked irritated, and I wondered if she'd heard of it either. 'Chan, Chan ...' My mother was trying to make social connections. 'The only Chan I know is that politician chap.'

Lucille laughed. 'That's my uncle, Cedric. And I agree, the less said about him the better.'

'I couldn't possibly comment. It wouldn't be fair to judge local politicians by Westminster standards.'

'Uncle Cedric is descended from a long line of Hong Kong crooks who could run rings around any old Westminster system.'

Two little pink circles appeared on Mum's cheeks. 'I wouldn't know about that ...'

Lucille turned to me. 'We'd better get down to Pearlie's before she closes for lunch.'

Her Mini Moke bumped along a dirt road, past the higgledy-piggledy trade stores and fibro shacks of Chinatown, until she pulled up in a dusty gutter. A gang of teenagers hung around the front of the pool hall and a few called out a greeting. She waved a film star ta-ta, and led me up a metal staircase that ran up the outside of the building, her heels clanking all the way.

Lucille introduced me to Pearlie, a plump Chinese

lady in a caftan who ushered us into a windowless room stuffed with racks of clothes. She and Lucille greeted each other with hugs and a lot of chattering in Chinese. Every so often during the conversation Pearlie would look me up and down; they were talking about me and making no attempt to hide it. I looked around at the clothes and my heart sank. They were what my mother would call frocks, and what's worse, she would have approved of them.

Pearlie held up a dress covered in cherries and Lucille nodded her approval. I was struggling to think how to say it wasn't for me, when Lucille disappeared behind a curtain and I realised we were there on her behalf.

There were an awkward few minutes while Pearlie and I exchanged looks. She made no attempt at conversation, and I wondered if she spoke any English. At last Lucille pulled the curtains back with a flourish.

'I love it, I do.' She twirled. 'But perhaps it's too busy?'

I was feeling more and more like a child amongst the grown-ups, when Lucille finally announced it was time to go. After more hugs and laughter, Pearlie folded me within her billowing sleeves and said something over my shoulder.

'She likes you,' Lucille explained. 'And she's a good judge.'

I left with the feeling that I'd just been through some kind of vetting process.

Back in the Mini Moke, Lucille sat for a few moments before turning to me. 'I need to ask you something, Billie. *Some* white girls, they chase Errol because he's different but that's all they're interested in. Tell me you're not like that.'

My cheeks burnt. 'Of course not.'

She hugged me so tight I could smell her patchouli oil and I was glad she couldn't see the guilty look on my face.

Hidden in the depths of our garden was a Japanese concrete bunker from the Second World War. It was cut into the hillside and so well covered by twisting vines that it wasn't visible until you almost stumbled upon it. A set of steps led down to a shadowy antechamber, and by the time you reached the main chamber, you could barely see your hand in front of your face.

When I was younger, my friends and I had played chicken in the bunker, daring each other to stay alone in the dark with the ghosts of long-dead soldiers. So, it made perfect sense that next time Errol came over, while my mother was at her regular golf morning, I took him there.

The lure of danger pulled me down the mossy stairs and into the darkness. Errol was right behind, his breath on the back of my neck. I stopped, waiting for him to touch me, but nothing happened. When I opened my eyes, he had moved further away.

'It's kind of dirty down here, isn't it?' he said.

Feeling foolish, I turned and retreated up into the daylight.

Errol followed and we hovered awkwardly next to the bunker. He seemed about to speak a couple of times before he mumbled something about going to the Imperial in Chinatown that night. 'Lucille said she could pick you up, the three of us go together?'

I was confused. Why was he asking me out when he didn't seem to want to take things further? Was it out of pity or to humour Lucille? I agreed anyway because I was curious – about the Chinatown cinema my sisters called 'the fleapit' – and his motivation.

I was still feeling confused when Lucille came to the door after dinner to fetch me. Mum frowned but Dad shrugged a kind of grudging approval so I jumped into the Moke before they could change their minds. Errol sat in the back seat looking sullen while Lucille chatted away, which didn't help.

The Imperial Picture Palace, painted the standard Chinatown shade of faded mildew green, looked more like a rundown church hall than a cinema. The posters on the billboard out the front advertised martial arts epics from Hong Kong and Hollywood westerns.

The place was packed, mainly with Chinese and local young people. Lucille left the two of us alone together when some friends called her over. Errol led me by the hand right through the middle of the crowd. Near the front were a couple of rows of old deckchairs all jammed together like a pit in front of the screen. We squeezed along one of the rows and fell together into a deckchair.

The smell of hot bodies and coconut oil was overpowering, and I leant my face into Errol's shoulder. I could feel his hipbone next to mine and I lay as still as I could, afraid he might pull away. That night was like a dream, floating skin on skin in a hammock suspended in the darkness, and I didn't want it to end.

The movie was about a hero freeing a village from a gang of thugs. In the climactic scene he spun a circle of white as his kicks rained down on the bad guys. There were shouts of 'Go, Bruce' and wolf whistles as he exchanged glances with the heroine. Like watching an opera, I could feel the emotions without understanding the words.

When the maiden rewarded her rescuer with a kiss, Errol ran a finger lightly across my palm and I felt every nerve tingle.

The screen flashed with light as the film ran off the spool and the glare from the overhead fluorescents flooded the room. I blinked my way to the exit, holding Errol's hand, feeling exposed. Just as we were about to slip into the welcoming night, someone called out his name.

A Chinese boy stood in the shadows next to the exit.

Errol wheeled around grinning. 'Hey, man, I didn't know you were home already.'

The two embraced.

Errol turned to me. 'Billie, this is Desmond.'

The boy seemed to step back rather than forward as Errol introduced me. His eyes were down, his face flat as a mask. He kept his hands behind his back as though I had something contagious and nodded without meeting my eyes.

Errol was still talking. 'Desmond's kind of a cousin, but we're more like brothers …' He patted Desmond's arm.

I couldn't understand why this boy was ignoring me and why Errol didn't seem to notice.

'I've got to get Billie home before she turns into a pumpkin,' he continued. 'See you soon, man.'

On the way home, I tried to recapture the moment when Errol had traced his finger across my hand, but Desmond had broken the spell.

Every day dawned hotter than the last, and my saggy old bathers were becoming an embarrassment. I found Mum's sewing basket and started pulling out scraps of material.

Rosie stuck her head around the corner. 'Whatcha doing?'

'I'm going to make some new bathers. My old ones are just about gone in the bum. I thought maybe I could use your new bikini as a pattern.'

I braced myself for a mean comment but instead Rosie smiled. 'Why don't I help you? You need some decent material first, though. Try Chinatown.'

The Chinese had always seemed like outsiders in this country; shopkeepers resented by the locals and looked down on by the whites. But after my trip to Pearlie's, I realised that in Chinatown I was the outsider. I ducked into the first decent-looking trade store. 'Wu Trading Emporium' was painted in elaborate gold lettering above its entrance.

Turned out the word 'emporium' was misleading; inside, the store looked the same as all the others. The floor was concrete, and every corner was crammed with stuff. An island of glass cabinets was filled with watches, jewellery and transistor radios. Above the cabinets hung assorted lengths of material and blouses and shirts in fluorescent tropical patterns, and in the far corner dried fish were skewered on hooks. The tops of the cabinets were lined with jars filled with the exotic treats of my childhood – brown, wrinkled salty plums and garish strips of red pickled ginger.

A shadow appeared behind the island counter and suddenly Desmond was standing in front of me. He looked like he'd been caught out. 'What are *you* doing here?'

'It's a free country, isn't it?' I tried to sound breezy, but I was wondering what I'd done to upset this boy.

He blushed golden peach. 'I'm sorry, I didn't mean to be rude. I'm an idiot sometimes.'

'Errol told me you got a scholarship to Grammar, so you're definitely not an idiot.'

'Just … in social situations.' He blushed a bit more.

'Don't worry about it. Hopefully you can help – I need some material.'

The display rack of fabric was jammed in a corner. Our bodies were so close I had to lean back to avoid touching him.

'How much do you need?' he asked.

It was my turn to blush. 'I'm making some bathers. So not much.'

The flicker of a grin moved across his lips. He held up a hibiscus print in turquoise and green. 'I think these are your colours.'

He wrapped the length carefully in brown paper and string.

'Do you work here often?' I asked, to fill the silence.

'Only every day.'

'Don't you get bored?'

'It's just what my family does.'

'Well, I hope they give you some time off.'

I hurried out the door, in case he thought I was flirting.

# Chapter 5

## Vanessa

Mum talked about Susan coming home all week and my heart sank a little further with each mention. Rosie had been okay this holiday, but as soon as Susan arrived, she'd drop me. My sisters didn't have a lot in common; they just had more in common with each other than they had with me.

They were away at boarding school together for two years before I joined them, and they had formed a close unit I couldn't break into. It didn't help when I was suspended for climbing over a neighbour's fence to get back into school after the gates were locked. Susan, who was Head Prefect, had to plead my case with the headmistress.

I can still hear Miss Carmichael's snooty tone: 'You

may be allowed to act the savage in New Guinea but down here we expect our *gels* to behave like ladies.'

Susan glared at me and I knew she was thinking that Mum would be mortified. As it happened, she was able to convince Miss Carmichael not to tell our parents, but that meant I was in my sister's debt. It seemed to give her permission to treat me like a child.

Rosie wasn't much better. 'Maybe you'll stop acting like a boy when you start looking like a girl.'

My classmates wanted to know why I was called Billie. 'Isn't it a boy's name?' they'd ask. A kind adult once told me about Billie Holiday and sometimes I'd claim to be named after her, but I'd never heard any of her records played at our place. I guess my father had hoped for a son after two daughters and so I'd got Billie.

On Friday afternoon, we headed out as a family to the airstrip to welcome home Susan. Meeting the plane was a popular pastime in Kavieng and the airport was like a drive-in theatre. Cars pulled up in a line behind the low cyclone-wire fence just before the plane was due. People came to see who was arriving; they wouldn't even bother getting out of their car unless it was someone they knew.

My heart pounded when I saw Errol standing alone

further along the fence, and I was about to wave when he raised his eyebrows in my direction, barely an acknowledgement. My cheeks burnt in humiliation as I looked away.

A faded gold Bentley pulled up at the end of the line of Kombis and Mini Mokes. Nobody bothered with proper cars in PNG because they rusted too quickly – nobody except the plantation owners. The Bentley belonged to Don and Madeleine Barry.

Don and his sister, Sybil, had come to New Ireland from India after the war. Sybil married Roger Warwick, whose family owned most of the coconut plantations on New Ireland. Rumour had it that Don returned from a trip to Singapore with the mysterious Madeleine. Together the two families ran a string of plantations that stretched for mile upon mile of the coast road.

Don was shaped like a beach ball, and every few minutes he wiped sweat away with a large polka-dot handkerchief. Madeleine was fair and willowy, and her delicate wrists looked about to snap under the weight of her gold bracelets. She was dressed in nautical stripes that would be more at home on the French Riviera.

They were here to meet their daughter, Vanessa. Susan came down the stairway in front of Vanessa, and my sister's pale face and lank ponytail looked mousy in comparison. Vanessa wasn't just pretty, she was beautiful, and something about the way she flicked back her hair showed she knew it.

As soon as I saw Vanessa I remembered how much I hated her. Rosie had introduced us a few times, but each time she acted as though it was the first and spent the whole time looking around for someone more interesting. Now I had a new reason to hate her because I noticed Errol gazing at her from behind his sunglasses.

I hugged Susan, all the time watching Errol over her shoulder. He moved up to wait in the area where the baggage trolley would be left, although he clearly wasn't waiting for any baggage. Vanessa sidled up next to him and they stood facing the same direction, like strangers, as they exchanged a few words out of the corners of their mouths. Then Don and Madeleine joined Vanessa and Errol moved gently away.

On the drive home, I wound down the window and leant into the breeze to block the sound of my sisters' chatter. Errol's indifference at the airport had stung, but maybe he'd done it for my own protection? Like any small town, Kavieng was full of gossip. Perhaps he and Vanessa were just friends; even friends had to be careful, didn't they?

After a roast chicken dinner in honour of Susan's homecoming, Rosie put on her sweetest voice and said, 'Mum, can we girls go to the flicks at the club? The Barrys will be there and I bet the Warwicks will be too.'

My sister knew exactly how to appeal to Mum's snobbery. She was desperate to have us mix with 'the right people'. When I first got my period, she'd warned me against spending time with 'native' boys. She couldn't see that Rosie was in way more danger from the clean-cut private school boys at The Kavieng Club.

As we walked into the club that night, the old Raj look of heavy dark timber and rattan armchairs contrasted with the rows of orange plastic chairs arranged in front of a pull-down screen.

Vanessa was nowhere to be seen but Rosie didn't seem to care. She'd spotted the Warwick boys in the back row. They were shouting playful insults across at their uncle, Don Barry, who was overflowing one of the barstools.

The Warwicks called over to Rosie and she nudged Susan.

'We really shouldn't leave her.' Susan nodded in my direction.

'Billie hates boys. She'll be fine.'

As Susan stood undecided, Lucille and a group of kids walked in. Lucille waved at me. I hadn't known whether my friends from Chinatown would be there or not; despite no explicit race restrictions, not many of the non-white community were brave enough to front.

'It's okay.' I nodded to Susan and she followed Rosie. Don passed a tray of drinks over to the boys. I smiled. Let Susan discover the charms of the Warwick boys for herself.

I began to move along a row of seats towards Lucille when the lights dimmed and I sat down where I was. The crowd started to call out the countdown as the grainy numbers flashed up on the screen.

'This seat free, miss?' It was Errol's playful tone, right next to my ear. As he sat down next to me, he patted my thigh.

My heart was thumping. The silence between us grew as all the noises – the chants, the laughter, the scraping of chairs – receded into the dark. Was I supposed to act like I hadn't noticed anything at the airport earlier? I wished I'd listened when girls at school were talking about boys.

The movie was *The Go-Between*. A lot of smouldering looks passed between the blonde aristocrat and her dark tenant farmer before they were caught in the hay together. The farmer beat the rich boys at their own game in the village cricket match, while his lady swooned on her deckchair. Something about the way her collarbones bobbed beneath the lace of her dress made me think of Vanessa.

I stole a glance at Errol, who sat arms crossed, staring straight ahead. Of course, the beautifully wayward blonde survived, while her lover did the honourable thing and put a bullet in his head.

I knew I should have pitied the farmer, but any fool could see that lady of the manor was a phony. How could you love someone and be ashamed to be seen with them? The young kid who'd acted as their go-between was the one I felt for – he was totally out of his depth.

As the credits rolled, a Chinese man strode down the passageway between the rows of seats and the glare from the projector picked him out like a spotlight. It was hard not to stare; in a white safari suit, he was a dandy from the twisted ends of his handlebar moustache right down to his shiny boots. They were made from some kind of mottled material that looked like white snakeskin. It had to be Cedric Chan.

Errol stiffened as the man passed our seats. We watched him approach the bar, which was covered in palm thatching, like an amateur production of *South Pacific*.

'Mr Chan,' Don said. 'Didn't know we'd be honoured by our local member. What's your pleasure?'

'We heard you like a beer,' someone said. Laughter cracked around the bar.

Cedric Chan flinched. 'Johnny Walker on ice. Black label, if you're buying, Don, *old chum*.'

'I've got to go.' Errol's voice in my ear made me jump.

'But I thought …'

He hissed. 'I hate this place. At uni I feel like a human being, but once I'm back here …'

He stood and walked purposefully towards the bar. I stared after him, stung by his anger.

Cedric Chan was exiting the throng, carrying his Scotch aloft. Errol stopped dead in front of him. The slightest flicker of recognition crossed Cedric's face, before he sidestepped Errol with a click of his Cuban heels. It was the perfect brush-off.

Errol stayed on the spot for a full second before he turned and disappeared into the darkened interior of the club. I could only see the back of his head, but I felt the hurt in that hesitation. I was out of my seat before I had time to think.

I caught sight of him at the end of the corridor and then he suddenly vanished. I peered around the corner into the shadows and saw nothing but rows of closed doors and a sign that read 'Guests only'.

A cold hard feeling in my gut told me Vanessa was behind one of those doors, that Errol had just snuck into her room.

Competition had never been my thing. I shied away from most sports at school. I loved to swim, but during races I pretended I was alone in the water. In my head, my lane was the only lane in the pool. When I turned out of the water to breathe and heard the screams of the crowd, I couldn't wait to retreat back into the silence.

So, I fled without a backward glance, only remembering my sisters when I was outside. I waited in the shadows, thoughts spinning through my head. If Errol hated the club so much, why had he been sneaking around its corridors? And why didn't he hate Vanessa? She and her family *were* the club.

# Chapter 6

## On patrol

When Dad invited me to an island down the coast the following Monday, I jumped at the opportunity. I had always loved going out into the bush or onto the water with him. When I was younger my mother and sisters had sometimes come under sufferance, but Dad didn't bother asking them now. It was just him, his men and me, and there was a satisfying sense of purpose uniting us all. We were not just travelling: we were on patrol.

'Let's walk down.' Dad led me through the garden. The hour just after breakfast is a magic time in the tropics. The sun is coaxing the world out of its bed; it hasn't begun to beat down on it yet. We strode along the road towards the wharf, the crushed coral surface crunching under our feet.

'It's a beautiful island we're heading to,' Dad said. 'Be more like a cruise than a patrol.'

'You must have a reason for visiting, though?'

'Just a minor disagreement between the villagers and Humpty Dumpty.' He saw my confusion. 'That's Mr Barry to you. The island we're going to is just across the water from the Barry plantation.'

Hopefully Vanessa was still in town and we wouldn't run into her.

Dad's snowy-haired driver, Julius, was waiting at the wharf with the large metal box Dad always took on patrol. In Dad's early days in New Guinea, back before I was born, it had been carried up and down mountain tracks on a pole between two carriers.

The crew was up on deck, getting ready to leave. The morning sun intensified all the colours – the whitewash was whiter, the brass gleamed brighter, the gloss of the wooden planks shone deeper than I had ever seen them. The 'boss boy' wore a traditional black-and-white *lap-lap* with an anchor insignia, but the younger crewmen had gone for more practical King Gee shorts, so I wouldn't have to avert my eyes when they cast off.

The captain of the trawler was one of Dad's old-timer mates, Max. He looked like a bulldog with a suntan, and growled orders out in a Dutch accent. I used to be scared of him before I discovered his bark was much worse than his bite.

Dad nodded at Max but didn't speak as Max took up his position on the other side of the wheel.

I loved my father's silences. As a child, I'd follow him around and at the end of the day I'd get my reward. I'd wait out on the seesaw at the back of whichever club or bar we were at for him to bring me a root beer to match his South Pacific. We'd click our glasses, 'Cheers'. He'd sit next to me and we'd listen to the music floating down from the window, the Beatles maybe, or Chuck Berry. I knew when Dad just wanted to sit – Mum could never get the hang of that.

'Morning, Miss Billie.'

It was Sergeant Eugene, the head of the local police force in New Ireland and one of my favourite people. He stood at the front of about half a dozen policemen. They marched on board in their blue shirts and shorts, silver badges shining on their slouch caps.

Sergeant Eugene was straight and strong like a tree trunk. He came from New Britain, where the people were proud. The government liked to post senior policemen away from their home province to avoid conflicts of interest, so New Britain's loss was our gain.

I saluted. We enjoyed playing a game of mock formality with each other.

Dad didn't greet Eugene directly. Instead, he said, 'My escort's here, Max. Let's cast off.'

It was only as we got under way that I wondered why he needed a police escort.

The trawler kept parallel to the shore until we rounded the point and then headed out to avoid the shallow reef that ringed the coastline of New Ireland. The water, pale aquamarine above the coral, turned an inky blue as we moved into open water.

We picked up speed and the trawler shuddered and shook as it was lifted by the swell. I wasn't the best sailor and the diesel fumes were hard to escape in the cabin so I went down to the little deck at the stern. Eugene was trawling a fishing line over the side. The engine noise made it impossible to speak so we grinned at each other. I hadn't been sure how I'd feel to be out on patrol with Dad again, but Sergeant Eugene's grin reassured me.

Walking back towards the wheelhouse, I heard Max's raised voice. 'You can't tie my whole crew up just to take your girl on an outing. It's not the old days anymore. I have to account for my diesel.'

Dad's voice was soft but steely. 'These land disputes can

turn ugly so I need some police, but driving them down in a truck and then having to ferry them across a couple at a time in Don's little speedboat … it'd send the wrong message. We need to arrive as one united force.'

A huge monster of a container ship appeared off our ocean side. When I was small the local boys had taught me to weave little boats out of coconut fronds, which we pushed out into the current. That was how we must look to the people on the bridge of that ship, as insignificant as a tiny toy tossing in their wake.

I knocked on the window of the wheelhouse and pointed towards it.

My father came out grinning. 'Don't worry, Billie. That's miles away. It just looks close because it's so bloody big.' He pointed down to the blue-black water. 'Once you're outside the reef, the seabed falls away. This channel could be hundreds of feet deep.'

We kept the New Ireland coastline within sight as we chugged south for a couple of hours. Then a line of coconut palms emerged from the waves. It must be the island. Bigger than Nusa, it looked to be only a short distance from the mainland.

'Where's the Barry's place?' I asked Dad.

'That's their copra shed.' He pointed to a building on

the shore. 'The plantation goes on for miles, but the house itself is that one up on that hill.'

'The island's so close.'

'Too close. Don's always treated the islanders like his personal slaves, except some of them don't want to play anymore.'

The trawler's engine dropped an octave as we approached a wooden jetty. The engine then screamed into reverse and the crew shouted commands at each other. Sergeant Eugene stood silent at the head of his men.

A crewman jumped onto the jetty and dropped the heavy woven ring of rope around the bollard in one fluid movement. The gangway slapped down onto the wooden planks and the dull throb of the engine stopped, leaving an eerie silence. For a moment, it seemed as though the island was deserted.

Sergeant Eugene marched along the jetty ahead of his men and they took up a position on the sand with their backs to us, like guards.

My father strode behind them as though he was midway through a game of golf, relaxed but purposeful. A small man with a limp emerged from under a tree and shuffled towards him. He wore a silver councillor's badge on his white shirt and there were grey streaks in his hair.

They embraced and Dad pointed to me. 'Piccaniny number three bilong me. Billie, this is Mister Tobias, number one man bilong island.'

I bent my head in an awkward gesture of respect.

Tobias shook his head and gave a strange smile. 'No. Mipela no number one man. Masta Bill emi number one man yet.'

He was saying my father was still in charge.

Dad put his hand on the man's shoulder. 'Mi bigpela sori meri bilong yu i-dai pinis.' He turned to me. 'Poor fellow's wife died only a few months ago. They'd been married forty years – that's right isn't it, Tobias?'

The little man nodded, wiping his eyes with the back of his hand.

'Bigpela sori.' Dad rubbed his hands on his pants. 'But right now, we need to get on with business. Are the men ready?'

Tobias nodded. We began our slow procession; Dad first, his arm supporting Tobias, then Eugene and his men, shortening their stride so as not to kick the old man's bare feet with their boots, and lastly me, dawdling behind.

As we walked, I became aware we were being followed. It was normal for a gang of kids to trail along behind us when we arrived anywhere, but these boys looked older than usual and they were shadowing us, sliding in and out of the shady patches under the trees like phantoms. It was starting to unnerve me until the one at the front of the pack winked at Sergeant Eugene and he winked back.

Soon we arrived at the village, which was set back a little from the beach. Small huts were arranged in a circular pattern around a clearing. An avenue of cannas lined the path to a central hut without walls that was much larger than the others. At that moment, a breeze fluttered and the flowers swayed backwards and forwards like welcoming orange flags on long purple stakes.

A couple of thin dogs lying on the ground jumped up as Dad and Tobias walked by. One of Eugene's men kicked out as he took up his position beside one of the posts, and the dogs skulked away.

About twenty island men sat around a large wooden table in the middle of the hut. They looked as though they had been scrubbed clean, but the smell of campfires lingered in the air.

The boys who had been following us joined the audience of women and children sitting in a wide circle outside the hut. I leant against a post behind Sergeant Eugene, trying to be inconspicuous.

Tobias began an elaborate welcome. 'Mr DC, Masta Bill …'

Dad shook his hand above his head impatiently. 'Don't beat around the bush, Tobias. Your people are unhappy and I want to know why. What has Masta Don done to upset you?'

'Maybe I can explain.'

I couldn't see the speaker, but I didn't need to. I'd have known that voice anywhere. I instantly pictured his heavy eyes, lazy grin, glossy skin.

# Chapter 7

## Masta Don

My face was hot, my mind racing. I couldn't believe I'd somehow stumbled into Errol's village. He hadn't mentioned he lived on an island, had he? I wanted to sneak away before he saw me but how do you sneak off an island?

'Don Barry steals our coconuts,' Errol said. 'My people used to take them over to that big shed of his in exchange for a bag of rice or sugar. But we won't accept peanuts anymore. He says the trees are his and we're still his kanakas.'

At the mention of the insult *kanakas*, faces around the table were anxious.

'Who exactly are *your* people?' Dad asked.

I didn't have to see Errol's face to know he'd be wearing that same hurt look he had when he told me about his father.

'My name is Errol. I was born on this island.'

'Then Tobias is your chief, and he's the one who should speak for *your* people. Whaddaya say, Tobias?'

'Masta Don, emi friend bilong yumi. Emi lukaut good long mi.'

'So, Tobias is happy to let Don keep using the land,' Dad said. 'Hands up who agrees with him.'

Most of the older men's hands went up, a bit less than half the group.

'Nupela man, man bilong trade store – emi cam na stealim money belong yumi.' Tobias was talking about Cedric Chan, saying if anyone was stealing from them, it was the trade store, and by implication Errol's mother.

'This is bullshit,' Errol said.

The muscles in Sergeant Eugene's face tightened.

'Take a good look at the two of us, Mr DC, at your man Tobias and me,' Errol said, 'and ask which one can better speak for these people?'

'Tobias looks like he's still got the numbers.'

Dad was seeing things the way he wanted to see them.

There was a rustle of movement as Errol stood and I caught a glimpse of his angry profile as he marched out the other side of the hut. The younger men around the table also stood and left as well as the boys who'd followed us.

The older men who had stayed looked to Dad for guidance.

'That boy's a bighead,' Dad said, 'but he's all talk. Stick with Tobias and I'll help you sort out an agreement with Don.'

As we left, Dad called Tobias out into the sunshine. 'I know the boy's a pain in the arse, but you shouldn't insult his father.'

Tobias stood stony-faced.

'Now I better go and see what Don has to say for himself.' Dad glanced at his watch. 'If I can tear him away from his lunch.'

We left in formation, Sergeant Eugene up front with Dad, then me, and then the other policemen, a polite few steps behind. The sergeant looked proud and it struck me that his favourite position was beside my father.

My chest tightened as we approached the jetty, for standing next to it was a pack of young men, and in the centre, leaning back against an outrigger canoe, was Errol. He was wearing a rugby jumper with 'Queensland State Training Squad' across the front. His eyes followed me as we passed but he said nothing. I was feeling relieved but then his voice rang out, 'You know the old man's losing it, don't you, Mr DC?'

Dad wheeled around. 'That's Mister Cleary to you. And you would say that, wouldn't you?'

'Ask him about the little cult he's started.'

'Whaddaya mean by that?'

'The old fellow lost his marbles when his wife died. It's not just cargo he's after this time. He wants to bring his wife back to life. They've built a new spirit house. Deep in the bush back there, where they know you won't go.'

Dad weighed his words. 'Sounds like you're trying to make trouble.'

Errol shrugged. 'Believe what you like. I just don't want to see you taken for a fool.' He turned towards me. 'So, what do you think of my island, Billie?'

'What's that to you?' Dad snapped.

'Just want to make sure our guest's happy.'

The boys next to Errol grinned like it was a joke but he looked at me as though he was speaking in a code I'd understand.

Dad placed his hand on my shoulder. 'Come on, girl, time we were off.'

I spoke under my breath as we walked, 'You're not going to ask the old man? About the cult?'

Dad also spoke quietly, 'And make him think I don't trust him? That'd be playing right into that ratbag's hands.'

My legs were wobbly as I stepped back onto the trawler. Sergeant Eugene had taken up the same spot he had on the journey out, wearing a carefully neutral expression.

Dad said nothing until we were about to dock at Don's pier.

'Cocky so-and-so. You want to be careful of that boy. How does he know your name?'

'He sat next to me on the plane.' I tried to keep my voice steady. 'I didn't know …'

'Obviously not. State Training Squad be buggered.'

Don stood at the end of his pier, which was bigger than the one on the island. He was wearing a white planter's hat and his shorts billowed around his fat knees in the sea breeze. Two muscly local men in matching dark *lap-laps* stood behind him.

He pumped my father's hand before turning to me. 'This young lady must be Billie. Don't they grow up fast.' His shake was damp and squishy, but his blue eyes were sharp. 'I trust you'll take a bite of lunch with us?'

Dad shook his head. 'Kind of you but the crew caught some bonito on the way down and the cook's already filleted it. Wouldn't want to disappoint him.'

'Madeleine will be sorry she missed you.'

Dad nodded towards the island. 'Wouldn't want them to think I'm taking sides. Can we talk down here somewhere?'

Don pointed to the wooden shed next to us. We walked to the open sliding door and peered in. A waft of musty coconut caught in the back of my throat. There was a desk just inside the door. Don took the chair behind it and pointed Dad to a nearby trunk. I leant on the outside of the door.

I wished I could have snuck back to the island. I had so many questions for Errol. Was he angry with me or just with my father? Did the fight with Don have anything to do with Vanessa? And what exactly *was* going on between him and Vanessa?

Dad was speaking to Don. 'Things must be crook if you have to quibble over a few lousy trees.'

'It's the principle. Roger's grandfather planted those trees out there when all the islanders cared about was fishing. Now self-government's here and suddenly everybody thinks they're a landowner. If I give the plot back to the islanders, how many villages will claim pieces of my plantations? They won't be happy until they push me into the sea.'

'A land dispute's no good for anyone. Settle it.'

'I can't do that. It's not only me who stands to lose – it's all the plantation owners the length of this coast. Isn't it your job to keep the peace? You can start by arresting that mixed-race boy.'

'I presume you mean Errol. What law has he broken?'

'He's threatened to take the trees back by force. And he's pretty much turned the island against me. They say he's Cedric Chan's bastard and I believe it. He fights like a mongrel.'

'Yeah, well, he just accused Tobias of reviving the cargo cult.'

Don grunted. 'That was years ago, wasn't it, when they cleared land for the big planes that were supposed to bring in the cargo? Damned lucky they didn't clear the trees we're arguing over.'

'Nothing recent?'

'Nuh, I reckon the young fella's blowing smoke … where he shouldn't. He'd do anything to get control of that island.'

'Sounds familiar,' Dad said.

He stood up and the two men eyeballed each other. This time there was no hand shaking.

The smell of frying fish coming from the galley was overwhelming as we re-boarded the boat. Heading outside for some fresh air as we steamed along the channel, I looked up the hill towards the Barry house and saw a watching figure. I could make out just the vaguest outline, but I was certain somehow it was Vanessa, and it struck me that all that separated her from Errol was a five-minute boat ride.

# Chapter 8

## Cargo

'I don't understand cargo cults,' I said.

'You need to see the world through their eyes,' Dad said. 'White men arrived and with them all these *things* arrived, first by boat and then during the war by plane as well. Treasures like axes and spades and guns appeared like gifts from the gods. The local people figured that if they acted like white men, the cargo would come to them as well.'

'How do you mean, acted like white men?'

'Different cults did it differently – some made badges from tinned food labels while others built pretend radios from shells or carved wooden guns.'

'How could they believe those things could possibly work?'

'The key was faith. Like any religion. If they believed in the symbols strongly enough, the magic would work.'

He shouted back to Max in the wheelhouse, 'Can we go by Rudi's island? I need to pick his brains.'

About ten minutes later, we approached a tiny island. We dropped anchor a hundred metres offshore and Dad and I took the small speedboat from a hoist on the back over to the beach.

A man who looked like a beachcomber stood waiting on the sand. He was barefoot and wore the briefest of shorts. Every visible inch of his skin was tanned like leather and his silver hair was thick with salt. When Dad introduced me, he bowed.

'Rudi is a world expert on cargo cults,' Dad said. 'He came out from Sweden to study the cults here and never went home.'

The men drank cans of Carlsberg beer under the coconut trees. I lay on my stomach in the shallows and listened.

'Have you heard anything about a cult on Keriva, the island off Don Barry's place?' Dad asked.

'They had one after the war.'

'I'm talking right now.'

Rudi shook his head. 'I haven't heard anything, but it would make sense now, *ja*?'

'Why?'

'Self-government is here and independence is around the corner. Everything's in a state of flux and the old people will be frightened. They may feel they're losing control and try to use the old magic to get it back.'

'There's a young fellow out there who's a clear threat to the chief. Educated, charismatic, a right pain in the arse.'

Rudi pointed his finger at Dad in triumph. 'He'll be the catalyst for this.'

Dad shook his head. 'The young bloke's the one who pointed the finger, actually. I think he might have made the whole thing up to discredit Tobias.'

'Tobias … I know that name.'

'He's been the chief there for years.'

'Is he a little fellow? Never looks you straight in the eye?'

'That sounds like him.'

'He wasn't the chief then, though, more like a lieutenant.' Rudi put his hands up to his eyes. 'It's coming back to me now. When the cult was at its height, the chief suddenly died. And this Tobias became the chief. There was talk of sorcery.'

Dad grinned. 'When someone dies, sorcery always gets blamed. I don't believe in magic, Rudi, and nor do you.'

'But *they* do. And that's what matters. From what I can remember, Tobias was suspected but nothing could be proved. Be careful of that one.'

Dad laughed. 'Steady on, Rudi. Like I said, it's the young bloke *I* don't trust.'

I couldn't get Rudi's warning out of my head the whole trip back, even as we steamed into the safety of Kavieng Harbour. It was comforting to see our house emerging from the bush as we walked back up the hill, but I was still rattled. The aroma of mince tarts wafting from the kitchen didn't calm me.

Like most kids, Christmas used to be my favourite time of year. Parcels appeared magically at the end of my bed, containing toys like I'd never seen before. Then one year Susan let something slip and Mum confessed that there was no Father Christmas. *She* had ordered the toys months in advance from mail-order catalogues. She wanted me to see how much effort she'd made to keep the illusion alive. But all I saw, in a flash, was that the whole Christmas thing was a sham. The local boys I played with wouldn't be getting big parcels at the end of their beds. Probably not even small ones. It seemed such a waste of effort shipping up all the presents, frozen chooks and fake holly for so few.

The kitchen table was covered with trays of tarts in various stages of assembly. There was a patch of flour on Mum's forehead and she was rubbing her hands on her apron. She was in what she would call a 'flap'.

'I've just realised it's less than a week until Christmas,' she said to my father. 'We really need to get organised.'

'What's to organise?'

'I've invited those two new female teachers – they can't be on their own their first Christmas up here. And then there's Dan and Peter …'

'I'll leave that in your capable hands.' Dad winked at me.

'There's a card from Coogee on the table.'

Dad picked up the envelope and carried it silently into the dining room. We all knew what 'a card from Coogee' meant. Every Christmas my grandmother sent a Mass card that my father put into the sideboard unopened.

'What's a Mass card?' I'd asked Susan, when I was old enough to wonder.

'It's a card that promises a priest will say prayers for your soul.'

'Why does that make Dad grumpy?'

'Because it's only for him, silly. Grandma Eileen doesn't bother with our souls. She thinks we're going straight to hell.'

'That's awful.' I shivered. 'Why would she think that?'

'Because we're C of E and she's Catholic.'

'What's C and E?'

Susan groaned. 'Never mind. All you need to know is that a long time ago Dad's parents made him choose between Mum and them. And he chose Mum.'

Dad was on the plane to Port Moresby the next morning. He'd been summoned for a briefing about what was happening on the island. As Dad disappeared out the door, he explained that the 'office johnnies were jittery'.

Mum and I had a couple of fruitless trips to meet the afternoon plane before he finally turned up on the third day. He came down the metal stairs after the rest of the passengers, just as I was turning away. It took a few seconds for me to recognise him because he'd abandoned his usual khakis for long pants and a business shirt.

Back home we sat on the verandah with our cold drinks. He stretched back on his favourite old armchair.

'Jeez, it's good to be out of that rat hole. The day I get transferred to Moresby is the day we *go finish*.'

'Did it go badly then?' Mum asked.

'No worse than I expected. Everyone's paranoid about self-government. The politicians can't wait to get out of this country. Some of the stories you hear, you can see why.'

'Like what?'

Dad shot a cautionary glance at me.

'Come on, Dad, you can tell me.'

'Just a lot more unrest than there used to be. Break-ins, brawls, that sort of thing.'

'Thank God we live somewhere peaceful,' Mum said.

'The pen pushers told me to go easy on Errol, too. Apparently, he's the kind of person they want to encourage – can you believe that? All the loyal old men are going to be thrown on the scrap heap – including yours truly.' Dad laughed. 'They haven't got rid of me just yet though.'

# Chapter 9

## Christmas Day

The Anglican church was a stuffy wooden building with an almost exclusively white congregation; most of the locals went to the much bigger Catholic Church in the heart of Chinatown or the Adventist Hall on the far side of the airport.

Sweat was running down my thighs by the time the minister raised his voice. 'Only the Son of God can bring you the great riches of eternal life.'

He pointed to the nativity scene beside the pulpit. Three brown figures held out chests of gold tinsel to a pink-cheeked Jesus doll.

I thought about Tobias and the islanders as the minister droned on about the riches that await us in heaven.

Who could blame them for trying to get their hands on some of that cargo right here on earth?

As we finally walked back out into the sunshine, someone called to my father. It was Mister Sid, the chief medical officer, an Englishman with a pencil moustache and a posh accent.

'I say, Bill, isn't your eldest doing nursing? One of the doctor boys down at the nuns' clinic came off his motorbike and they could really do with a hand. Just dressings, that sort of thing. Think you could handle it, young lady?'

Susan agreed, of course. Duty was her middle name.

Mum had one condition. 'Just make sure you get her back for my New Year's Eve do, Sid. She's my right hand, you know.'

Back at our house, the atmosphere was subdued. Mum had asked two unmarried patrol officers and a bank clerk to join us, and they all arrived punctually in pressed shirts, shorts and a waft of aftershave. The bank clerk's shirt was violently swirling purple, the top two buttons open to reveal a gold chain floating on a mat of dark hair. He winked at Rosie as they were introduced, and Dad growled under his breath about 'bloody Casanovas'.

When the two female teachers arrived half an hour late, one of them joked about her hangover. I don't think

Mum would have invited these girls if she'd spent any time at all with them because they were what she would have called 'unsuitable'. They had on large loop earrings, and the dark-haired one wore a dress that exposed her midriff between what looked like curtain rings. She thrust a bottle of Porphyry Pearl at my mother and then upset her by asking for a beer instead of the dry sherry offered.

'Sydney girls.' Mum retreated to the kitchen with a shake of her head. She was no doubt thinking that these were the kind of girls she had saved my father from.

The clutch of men stepped out from the corner and soon the group was laughing, sculling drinks and scoffing the smoked almonds my mother saved for this special day. Mum emerged from the kitchen flushed, a row of sweat beads glistening on her upper lip.

We followed her into the dining room, which we only used on special occasions. The pictures on the wall were government issue – the familiar portrait of the Queen as a young woman and a black-and-white aerial photograph of Kavieng Harbour. A small revolving fan in the corner barely fluttered the paper chains draped around the room, and the vague smell of mothballs rose from plastic holly sprigs.

Tahl and Suriwan brought in steaming platters of roast chicken and vegetables and laid them on the white tablecloth between red and gold crackers.

'What a spread,' Dad said. 'You've excelled yourself this year, love.'

Mum beamed.

He began to carve the chickens while she passed around the roast vegetables and steaming gravy boats and we all filled our plates. One of the clerks had started his meal when my mother cleared her throat pointedly and Dad did a rushed grace. Crackers were popped and coloured paper hats donned. Conversation stayed polite until plates were cleared and wine glasses freshened. The women had already finished the Porphyry Pearl and moved onto Mateus Rosé. They fanned themselves with the holly sprigs and giggled.

Mum turned to Tahl. 'Bring in the children.'

Tahl held the door open and his children shuffled into the room from the kitchen. They came in birth order; the eldest, a girl of about ten, first; her younger sister, in a matching floral shift, next; and lastly the little boy in a short-sleeved shirt with his collar tightly buttoned. Their skin shone and they smelt of Velvet soap.

'Come closer,' my mother commanded.

They finally raised their eyes as they edged forward.

Mum bent down under the table and pulled out a pile of shiny packages with a flourish. 'Merry Christmas, children.'

The girls got small bottles of Seven Eleven cologne and the boy a soap on a rope. He held it up in puzzlement, spinning it like a top. Dad mimed washing under his armpits and the children laughed with relief. As they backed out of the room, Mum looked around with an air of self-congratulation.

Plum pudding was next, served with vanilla ice cream, which melted into a puddle almost immediately. Appetites were flagging, but the guests had moved onto claret.

The dark-haired Mona was laughing a little too loudly at one of my father's stories about Moresby bureaucrats when Mum turned to her. 'How do you find the native kiddies? It must be a bit of a shock after teaching in Australian schools?'

'The kids are great. But one or two of the local teachers are a bit prickly.'

'I can't say I blame them really,' the other girl said. 'We get twice as much money for the same job. That's what Gough Whitlam's going to get rid of.'

There was a long silence around the table before my father spoke. 'They've got to attract you girls up here somehow, don't they? What's going to happen when your mate Whitlam kicks us all out? How can a PNG government afford to pay *your* salaries to local people?'

'Bill, it's Christmas,' my mother said. 'Can't you leave politics at the office?'

'That's the problem with this bloody place. Everyone's got their head in the sand.' Dad turned back to the girls. 'Do you think Whitlam gives a damn what happens to this country? He's rushing the people towards independence whether they bloody like it or not. Everything we've done here might go down the toilet because he doesn't have the guts to see it through properly.'

There was a long silence.

My mother announced she had one of her headaches and excused herself. After she'd left, Mona suggested they play the game of Twister I'd got in my Christmas stocking.

Dad sat in an armchair with a mildly amused look as the young people got down on all fours. My sisters and I stayed on the sidelines, spinning the dial and making faces at each other. The bank clerk tried to get Rosie to join in, but my father shot him a warning glare.

There was a lot of giggling and groaning as bodies got enmeshed and collapsed together. The bank clerk sprawled on top of Mona.

'It's your turn, Bill,' she said. 'Why don't you show him how a gentleman plays the game.'

I could have sworn Dad blushed; something I'd never

seen before. He hesitated but after the other girl urged him on, he stood at the end of the mat like a gangly schoolboy.

'Take your shoes off, silly,' Mona teased.

Dad looked even more awkward as he leant down to undo his laces and the girls grinned at each other. Why did women always flirt with my father?

'Left hand green,' the clerk snapped.

My father bent forward and carefully placed his arm over Mona. She turned and thrust her chest forward and grinned up at him. He looked like a fly caught in a spider's web. I slipped out to the kitchen where Tahl was washing the dishes.

'Piccaniny i-go where?' I asked in slow Pidgin, holding out a handful of lollipops.

His face broke into a smile. 'Long haus.'

I walked to the side of the garden where a small fibro shed stood. We called it a house but it was so small it was really just a room for sleeping. All their family activities took place on the concrete verandah. They did their cooking on a single gas ring down one end and washed in a plastic sink set into a washstand on the other end, filled by bucket from the rainwater tank. Threadbare towels and tea towels hung from a clothesline strung under the corrugated iron roof.

Suriwan met me halfway across the lawn, the three children in tow. They each chose a lollypop and disappeared to quiet corners of the garden.

I wasn't comfortable playing the role of benefactor. Tahl and Suriwan had basically raised me. So many nights when Mum and Dad had gone out or entertained at home, Tahl had boiled us eggs with toast soldiers and Suriwan had sung us to sleep. The touch of her hand on my brow was more familiar than my mother's, but there was an awkwardness between us since I'd gone south to school.

Suriwan gestured towards the verandah, as though she sensed my discomfort and wanted to ease it. As I flopped down and leant back against the wall, an earthy smell brought back memories of hours passed here as a child, drinking bush tea and chewing sugarcane. She reached up and turned on the transistor radio and the air was filled with the tinny crooning of Bing Crosby roasting chestnuts on an open fire. She looked content and I wondered if she had any idea this would be our last Christmas together.

# Chapter 10

## New Year's Eve

'**M**um, tell Billie she has to come with me to the club to meet Vanessa,' Rosie shouted down the hall.

'Well, she could certainly do with more suitable friends.'

The thought of seeing the beautiful Vanessa again gave me a leaden feeling in my stomach but I knew I wouldn't be able to get out of it now. I complained the whole way there; I was being a bitch and I knew it.

'Vanessa's a snob.'

'How would you know?'

'Oh, I know.'

'But you've hardly spoken to her.'

'Yeah and that's how I want it to stay.'

Vanessa was nowhere to be seen when we got to the club so we waited by the entrance.

Rosie chatted on about a boy staying with Stuart, and I understood why she'd insisted I come along. She was trying to hook me up with one of her kind of boys.

After about twenty minutes, Vanessa sauntered up with two boys in her wake. She looked cool in a white cheesecloth shift that hugged her body in just the right places.

'Why are you waiting out here?' she asked.

She led us into a wood-panelled room marked Private Lounge and flopped down theatrically in one of several oversized wicker armchairs clustered around a round table. The large ceiling fan directly above blew the neck of her shift open to reveal the shadow of her left nipple.

She looked down but instead of adjusting her clothes she took a fluttering frangipani flower from behind her ear.

'Vanessa, you know Billie, don't you?' Rosie asked.

'Actually, I don't think we've been formally introduced.' She looked at me with more interest than I'd been expecting. 'But I know so much about you already.'

I felt myself flushing.

She held her hand out towards one of the boys. 'You know Stuart, I presume?'

Stuart and I acknowledged each other.

'And this is his friend …' She'd obviously forgotten the boy's name but instead of apologising she skipped right over him. 'Stuart, be a sweetie and get me a rum and coke.'

'I'm Damien,' the other boy said. I would have felt sorry for him, if he hadn't been looking down Vanessa's top quite so obviously.

'You were out early this morning,' he said.

Vanessa looked startled. 'How do you know that?'

'I knocked on your door to see if you were ready to go to breakfast.'

'I had something to do.'

'In this place?'

Vanessa leant over and picked up the frangipani flower that had fallen between us. 'I had to catch up with an old friend.'

Of course, the frangipani tree out the front of Lucille's. The flower was Vanessa's trophy, and she was letting me know it.

I stood up with a jerk. 'I've got to go.'

'We should get to know each other better,' Vanessa said. 'We've got so much in common.'

I was shaking as I walked away.

The next day was New Year's Eve. In the morning, an elderly nun in a Land Rover dropped Susan back as promised to help Mum get ready for her 'do'. After lunch Susan asked if Mum could spare her for an hour. 'Just for a quick dip.'

'As long as you take Billie with you,' Mum said. 'She's been getting under my feet lately.'

I stole a quick look in the mirror as I passed the bathroom in my new bikini. Desmond was right – turquoise was my colour.

The 'swimming pool' was a cage of metal bars fencing off a stretch of water on the foreshore. Some early administrator must have been nervous about sharks, although nothing more threatening than a reef shark had ever been seen in the harbour. A wooden boardwalk running around the top was great to jump off or loll around on.

As we walked up, I saw Errol's rusty Fastback parked under the trees. My stomach lurched. After the encounter on Keriva, I wasn't sure how he'd act towards me.

A single dark head was bobbing out next to one of the ladders. Susan headed directly out to that end of the boardwalk and I followed. She dropped her dress and dived straight in without acknowledging his presence. I undressed in an agony of discomfort. I felt his eyes on me but I followed my sister's example and dived straight in without looking.

I slowly came back to the surface with my eyes closed and then I felt hands lightly resting on my shoulders. I opened them and Errol's grinning face was about six inches from mine. He held my gaze and played with it, drawing it down to the shark's tooth hanging around his neck and back up to his eyes.

'I've been here three days straight trying to catch you, young Billie. And you know I don't really need to work on my tan.'

He released my shoulders and turned and dived underwater. His skin shone wet and tight like a seal's. A few feet below the surface there was a gap in the bars just wide enough for a person to squeeze through sideways. It was a favourite dare, to duck through and swim across to a concrete mooring post about ten feet away in the open water.

Errol resurfaced on the other side of the bars and beckoned to me. I moved to the bars and hung there, determined not to follow him into the deeper water.

'Why did you treat my father like the enemy?'

'I was just putting our case. We're supposed to have self-government but Don's still trying to steal our land. Your dad's the one acting like our enemy, looking after the white man's interests.'

'He's not, honestly. He was really tough with Don.'

'What did he say?'

Something about the way Errol was trying to sound casual pulled me up. 'How do I know I can trust you?'

'I thought we were friends, Billie.'

'And what about Vanessa? Is she your friend too?'

'You're jealous of Vanessa?' He laughed. 'Vanessa's a lost cause. You, on the other hand, are smart and your heart's in the right place – if only you'd see that Daddy's not always right.'

As he made this last point, he grabbed my strap through the bars and pulled me closer, until our faces were almost touching.

'Billie!' Susan's voice cracked across the water from the other end of the boardwalk.

I jerked my head back.

Errol's leg hooked around mine through the hole.

He spoke quickly. 'Lucille's having a party tonight. If you want to come, she'll pick you up.'

I nodded, barely moving my head, and swam back to the ladder. As I began to climb, I realised my legs had turned to jelly.

Susan got straight to the point. 'What were you doing with that boy, Billie? I bet he's got a reputation. His kind always do.'

I didn't react. I just hoped she wouldn't tell Mum. I was already working out how to convince her to let me go to Lucille's party.

Later, when I was getting dressed, Susan tapped on my door. 'Mum suggested I give you this.' She held out a lacy bra. 'I've grown out of it.'

'It's padded, isn't it?' I rolled my eyes.

'A tiny bit. And I thought you might need one of these.' She unfolded one of the cups to reveal a shiny condom packet. 'Don't look so shocked. I've been keeping Rosie out of trouble for years.'

My mother's party was in full swing by the time Lucille arrived, and she even seemed a little tipsy.

'Okay. Home by twelve thirty and be sensible.' Mum brightened. 'Oh, you've been invited to Vanessa's birthday party next Saturday. Now that will be a real party!'

Lucille waved away my apology in the car. 'Hey, she doesn't mean to be rude, I know. As long as you and I understand each other.'

Crowds of people were standing around Lucille's garden, moving inside only briefly to retrieve bottles from eskies littering the kitchen floor. The mood was generous. Everyone smiled at me although I didn't recognise many.

Errol didn't seem to be there and Lucille scanned the crowd with an unsettled look.

Someone called my name from underneath one of the trees. It was Desmond.

'Hey, the material you sold me, it worked out well,' I said.

He smiled and it was like something was glowing inside him. A little answering spark went off inside me. There was a long silence before he held out a cigarette packet. 'Do you want one?'

I didn't smoke but it seemed like a peace offering so I took one. I leant towards his lighter and we stood together a little awkwardly. The first drag went straight to my head and I remembered why I didn't smoke. I let it burn down a bit before I squashed it under my sandal.

'Where's Errol?' I asked. 'He asked me to come and now he's not here.'

'That's Errol for you …'

The noise of a car engine skidding up the driveway made us turn. Out of Errol's rusty Fastback stepped Vanessa in a black jersey halter dress, as if she was arriving at a Sydney gala.

I stepped back into the shadows. Lucille was hurrying in our direction. 'Shit! What gives her ladyship the right to crash my party? I didn't score an invite to hers.'

My face must have given me away because she leant forward and hugged me, her fingernails digging into my bare shoulders. 'Oh, Billie, please don't be upset.'

'I just don't understand what he wants.'

'I don't think he does either. That girl's like poison – he just needs to get her out of his system.'

She teetered off in Errol's direction and I felt even more wretched.

I turned to Desmond. 'I have to go.'

He was still standing under the tree when I glanced back one last time.

It was so peaceful walking back down the hill and along the foreshore in the dark. Sporadic noises from different directions seemed to be getting louder, and I guessed it was midnight because all the noises merged into one big muffled, whooping wave of sound.

The party at home had broken up. Dad was out the front laughing with a knot of men and Mum was nowhere to be seen. I lay on my bed until I couldn't hear voices anymore and then I crept out into the garden. I knew I was a little drunk because I had to think about everything, as though I was looking down on my body and telling it what to do.

Something drew me towards the bunker, and I sat on the mossy concrete.

A voice called out my name from the shadows. I thought I must have been dreaming because it sounded just like Errol.

Then he spoke again and it was Errol, but he sounded like a kid who'd lost his favourite toy. 'Why'd you leave like that, Billie? I wanted to talk to you – why do you think I asked you?'

'Why did you ask me, when you knew you were going to bring Vanessa?'

'I didn't know I was going to bring her, but Vanessa tends to get what she wants. She likes playing with me – she left before midnight to go to some better party.'

'Oh, poor baby, no New Year's Eve kiss then? I'm sick of you two. No way am I going to her party to watch the two of you carry on.'

'I'm not invited – are you joking? I'm just a bit of fun she can tell her friends at Frensham about. She'd never be seen with me. Not anywhere *real* people would be.'

This was what Lucille had been talking about that day in the Moke.

My anger evaporated. 'I'm sorry ...'

Errol sank down next to me. He slowly laid his head in my lap and I stroked his hair. I smiled quietly to myself. Vanessa would never understand this.

# Chapter II

## Return to the island

'Billie, wake up.' Errol was standing over me shivering. The sun had started to lighten a corner of the sky. I looked towards the house. Nothing moved. Thank God for hangovers, I thought, as I turned and headed inside. But I forgot to hold the door and it slammed behind me.

The light from the kitchen split the dark hallway like a searchlight.

'Billie, is that you?'

My father stood in the doorway wearing a pair of loose shorts. I noticed for the first time that his chest was starting to droop. How long had he been standing there? Had he seen Errol? Putting his finger to his lips, Dad led me out to the verandah.

When we were seated on the old rattan chairs, he leant towards me and spoke quietly, 'What were you trying to prove staying out all night, Billie?'

'Dad, I didn't do anything, I swear …'

'Then who was that boy I saw sneaking away into the dark?'

'One of Lucille's cousins. We're just friends, Dad, honest.'

'I'd like to believe you, but you've got to see how it looks. With a boy of that kind …'

'What *kind* is that, Dad? You brought me up to take people as you find them. I know you think a hell of a lot more of Eugene than you do of any white man in this town.'

'But I don't ask him round to dinner, do I, because he wouldn't be comfortable. We respect each other's differences. I never thought *you'd* give me this kind of trouble, Billie.'

I was relieved Dad hadn't recognised Errol, but I felt a pang of guilt. I hadn't exactly lied to him but I hadn't told him the truth either.

He said I had to stay home until he said I could leave. I was grateful he didn't tell Mum. It would be easier to get around her as she always had a committee or two on the go.

Dad was quiet for the rest of the day. It was the first time we'd ever fallen out and I bent over backwards trying to get his forgiveness. I followed him around while he did chores and just before dusk he relented. 'Bugger it. You can have your "Get Out of Jail" card, if you come with me.'

Dad went surf fishing around the point from the town. He didn't catch much but that didn't seem to bother him; fishing was just an excuse to get out there. I often went with him and pottered around the rocks, sniffing about and coming back like a faithful dog.

I stood in the shallows and felt the wash bubble around my toes and rush back out to sea. Each splash made me screw my eyes up tight against the spray. My cheeks felt hot and my head was light. The night before was starting to catch up with me.

I stepped into the waves and leant forward to splash my face. The water was licking the bottom of Dad's shorts. I moved next to him, so close that our legs were nearly touching. We stood silently watching the burnt-out sun as it slid across the sky into the sea. I didn't need to look at him. I knew I was forgiven.

The next morning, I snuck into the bunker. It was cool and deliciously silent down there. I wanted to turn over the memory of those few hours with Errol in my mind, trying to decide whether they were a treasure or a trinket.

As I emerged back into the sunlight, blinking, I sensed I wasn't alone.

'This must be the best damn view in town.' My father was sitting on top of the bunker, looking out to sea. He spoke slowly as though it was a revelation.

He wasn't usually home at this hour, and I'd never seen him sitting in the garden before. He stood and dusted off his shorts as though he was leaving, but he continued to stand in that same spot, staring.

'Is something wrong, Dad?'

'I've had a tip-off about the island. Apparently that rugby lout and his gang are going to stop Don's boats landing.'

'Who told you? Was it Tobias?'

'That's not your concern.'

'Errol's my friend. If I come with you, maybe I could talk him out of this.'

'Things might get a bit hairy. I really don't trust that little bastard.' Dad bit his lip. 'Sorry, I didn't mean it like that …'

It was time to play the sympathy card. 'Please, Dad. You said this was our last Christmas here. I'm not going to get another chance to go out with you, am I?'

He was silent for a few moments. 'Well … I guess you can come for the ride. But I'm going to drop you off at Don's until I've seen the lie of the land. We better go tell your mother.'

We found her packing up Christmas decorations.

Her mouth was tight. 'I don't see why you have to take her everywhere.'

Dad kissed the top of her head. 'I promise I'll bring her back safe and sound.'

Max was gruff when we arrived on board. 'Something you're not telling me, boss?'

'I'm not sure myself,' Dad said. 'It's only a fishing trip at this stage.'

I smiled at Eugene, who was standing on deck with his men, but he had on his official face.

The trip down the coast was hushed. It may have been a fishing trip but nobody did any. The policemen all looked like they were on guard duty. Even Eugene had no time for me.

Wherever I went I felt out of place, so I ended up in one of the cabins. I lay on a bunk and closed my eyes. I started to drift back to New Year's Eve. It had been the sweetest sensation I'd ever had, the gentle pressure of Errol's head in my lap and the feeling that he actually needed me. I was lying there wrapped in a fantasy when the engines slowed to an idle. We were approaching the channel.

Being dropped at Don's wharf like a naughty child was humiliating. The trawler steamed across the channel without me, but I smiled dutifully as I waved goodbye. Don's men on the wharf didn't know what to do with me. They looked around as if searching for the *masta* to give them directions and then pointed to a path edged with white boulders that led up the hill.

The house at the top made our official residence look like a dump. It was built from huge blocks of whitewashed stone and a polished wooden verandah ran around the perimeter. The clang from the large brass knocker on the front door echoed as though there were a hundred rooms beyond.

A young village girl in a frilly *meri* blouse answered the door nervously. She shook her head. 'Missus emi no stap.'

'Vanessa?'

More head shaking.

'Masta Don?'

This time she pointed in the direction from which I'd just come.

A plan was forming in my head. It wasn't my fault if nobody was there to look after me. I'd just have to make my way back to Dad the best way I could.

Canoes of various sizes were pulled up on the beach.

'Me kisim missus i-go long island?' One of the planta-tion boys was gesturing between a speedboat tied up at the pier and the island.

I nodded coolly, not wanting to seem too grateful, in case he guessed that my father wouldn't be pleased to see me. I grew more and more nervous as the boat slapped across the waves and the island loomed before us. Up ahead the trawler was moored next to a fancy-looking cruiser, which I guessed was Don's. One of the trawler's crew on the jetty tied us up.

The scene on the shore was like a play with too many characters. The bit players were the dozen or so policemen, who stood rigid with their backs to us, and opposite them about fifty young islanders slouching around like football spectators. I remembered Don's prediction that the villagers might push him into the sea; if they really wanted to, there wouldn't be much the police could do to stop them.

Dad stood between the two groups with Sergeant Eugene beside him. Don was on the jetty side, bigger than ever in a billowing shirt, his finger making an angry point. Right at the centre was Errol, bare chest rippling above his rugby shorts, arms crossed and leaning back all relaxed, like he was at a picnic.

'I'll never give up my land, you little upstart,' Don spluttered.

'You better hope you get citizenship then, when independence comes. You'll have to give it back when we kick you out.'

'Ease up, boy,' Dad said.

'Don't call me *boy*.'

'I'll call you what I damned well like.' Dad's voice sounded hard and angry, like a stranger's. His eyes flitted back in the direction of the police and that's when he saw me.

'Billie, what the hell are you doing here?' There was a nervous edge to his anger.

'Nobody was there, so one of the boys brought me across.'

'Always a pleasure, Billie,' Errol said.

'This has got nothing to do with her,' Dad said.

'I wouldn't say that. Why won't you admit it's personal, this thing between you and me?'

'I don't know what you mean.'

'Just admit you saw me with Billie at New Year's and that's why you've got it in for me.'

Dad's mouth was open. He'd clearly had no idea.

Errol's lips curled into a knowing grin. He caught my eye and winked like it was all a private game. But I didn't understand the game and I didn't want to play.

The mob behind Errol leant forward, like the fight was

on. Dad stepped forward and pushed Errol hard in the middle of his chest. 'Don't you dare speak about my daughter like that, you gutless little bastard.'

'You can't push me around like the old days.' Errol gestured back to his supporters. 'These fellas are dying to get stuck in. Don't hand them an excuse.'

Don laid a hand on Dad's shoulder. 'I don't blame you for wanting to knock his block off. I'd be the same if he talked about Vanessa like that. But wouldn't it be much better to put him in the calaboose overnight to cool down?'

Dad blinked as though he'd just been shaken from a dream. He leant towards Don and lowered his voice. 'I'm sorry, but my hands are tied. The boy hasn't actually committed a crime, and I'm dealing with a whole new set of rules now. Believe it or not, the pen pushers in Moresby are on *his* side.'

Don looked shaken. 'Are you trying to tell me you're just going to abandon me to this mob?'

'Of course not. I'm here to keep the peace. But I need to be even-handed.' Dad looked around. 'Where's Tobias? He might be able to calm them down.'

Errol chuckled. 'Probably clearing his airstrip for the ancestors that will never arrive. You're just a bunch of old men living in the past ...'

Dad turned to Eugene. 'Sergeant, come with me. The rest of you men, stay here and secure the jetty.'

Dad looked at me. 'You're a damn nuisance, Billie, but you'd better come with us.'

I skipped to catch up with them. We came to a hut on the edge of the village and Dad called out for Tobias. The old man shuffled out, dressed like an ancient boy scout in a filthy battered cap with a silver badge pinned on it.

'Why are you wearing that old clobber, Tobias?'

'Me goodpela luluai, Masta.'

'We don't have *luluais* anymore, mate. I wish we could go back to the old days too, but today I need you to be *Head Councillor.*'

Dad gently removed the cap from Tobias' head and put it down on a log. Putting his hand on Tobias' shoulder, he led him down the path, without a backward glance. Eugene and I looked at each other.

'Was a *luluai* a kind of policeman?' I asked.

He snorted. 'Emi clerk tasol. Takim census, writim name.'

I remember the census books back in Dad's office, lists of people's names and ages that the village clerks had recorded.

Eugene carried the discarded cap to a wooden

cupboard next to the hut and was placing it inside when I heard him catch his breath. Peering into the dark interior, I saw a wooden statue about two-foot tall, decorated with black, white and orange lines. The head was a woman's but the body had a short puffed-out chest like a game bird. The cowrie shell eyes looked like they might spring open at any time.

'What is it?' I whispered.

'Malangan,' he whispered back. 'When someone die, people make malangan. Not just look like dead person, hold their spirit too.'

'This one's a woman?'

He nodded.

I shivered. 'Tobias' wife?'

Another nod.

'What's wrong, Sergeant Eugene?'

'Malangan belong in spirit house. Strongpela magic true.'

'Then we should tell Dad.'

Eugene looked uncomfortable. 'Masta no like mi tok tok magic.'

'Well, I'm going to tell him. Come on.'

As we walked away, I felt the beady shell eyes boring into my back.

The scene back at the jetty was more relaxed. The police stood around near the ramp, while Errol and his followers lounged under the trees. Don had retreated to his cruiser.

Dad and Tobias stood on the sand facing the islanders. Without the cap Tobias looked sensible, almost dignified.

Dad cleared his throat and spoke in a measured tone. 'I've had an *interesting* talk to your Head Councillor, Tobias. He tells me Mr Chan wants to muscle in on the arrangement your village had with Masta Don.' He looked directly at Errol. 'Pretty obvious why *you're* stirring up trouble against Don, isn't it?'

A murmur went through the crowd.

Errol jumped to his feet. 'That's a lie. At least … that's not why I'm doing it.'

'But the bit about Mr Chan's true?'

Errol shrugged. 'How should I know? I'm not his keeper.'

He slumped back into the shadows with his head down. The youths around him looked rattled.

Dad stepped forward until he was looming right over Errol. 'Don and his men come and go as they please, got it? Or I'll be back – and this time it *will* be personal.'

There was a hard edge to Dad's voice that shocked me. I wanted to protest but as Sergeant Eugene and his men fell in protectively around us, I saw we were a tiny white island in a sea of brown faces.

# Chapter 12

## Golf Club smorgasbord

Back on board, Dad got straight to the point. 'Time you and me had a little talk. What exactly has been going on between you and that ratbag?'

I felt my cheeks burn. 'You should treat him with a bit more respect.'

'Did he treat you with respect? Implying those things about you in front of everyone?'

I took a deep breath. 'It was the truth, Dad. It was him you saw leaving that morning. But I swear, nothing happened.'

'That's great, that is. You know he likes to wind me up and you stayed out all night with him anyway. Are you stupid, Billie, or do you really not care?'

Dad stormed off towards the wheelhouse before I had a chance to speak. I was stung by his words, but even more, I was stung by his refusal to let me explain. He'd never believe me now, whatever I said. It was so unfair.

And I couldn't figure out Errol. Why had he chosen to taunt Dad when Don had been standing right there? He'd done a lot more with Vanessa than he ever had with me.

I found Sergeant Eugene on the little deck at the stern, tossing an old cricket ball up and down in the air. I asked him if he had any kids.

'Yes, Miss Billie, onepela tasol.' He stretched his hands down next to his knees and I pictured the little head cradled there.

'You'd be a great dad.'

It came out sounding so much more patronising than I'd wanted. We were each playing a role and no amount of goodwill could bridge the gap between us. I really didn't know anything about Sergeant Eugene except I'd trust him with my life.

After what felt like hours, Dad came up and pointed out to the side. 'Look, they're our twin islands up ahead.'

'You're talking to me, then?'

'I shouldn't have lost my temper. But you've got to promise you'll stay away from that boy.'

I took a deep breath. 'Dad, I need to tell you something. Tobias has a *malangan* of his wife. In his house.'

'Does he, now?'

'Eugene told me it's powerful magic. He said it should be in the spirit house.'

'Eugene's a good policeman but underneath the uniform he's superstitious. The thing about magic is that it can only hurt you if you believe in it. And we don't.'

The harbour loomed up ahead, washed in the tangerine light of dusk. The trawler chugged past the headland where Dad liked to fish, then past his office until we finally reached the wharf and the swimming pool. Memories of lunchtime picnics and twilight dips came flooding back. This place was so precious to me and I stood to lose it all in the next year.

Mum called out as we walked into the house. 'You two better get cleaned up quickly. Remember, Bill, you asked Nathan and his wife to the Golf Club smorgasbord.'

She came out from behind the kitchen door, rubbing her hands across her apron. 'Damn crumbs won't stick to the chicken legs.'

Rosie and I grinned at each other. Mum normally said 'cursing' was a sign of bad breeding.

Dad tried to soothe her. 'Don't worry, darl. They'll still taste beaut.'

He didn't understand the importance of presentation at the Golf Club smorgasbord. Plates were decorated with doilies and garnishes so they'd empty quicker than their competitors.

'Maybe Tahl can rustle something up?' he continued.

Mum was outraged. 'But that would be *cheating*.'

A good golfer could have driven their ball from our front garden onto the first green of the Golf Club, that's how close it was. While The Kavieng Club was built on the grimy bones of an older German establishment, the Golf Club was all-Australian. The building had a temporary look about it as though it could be dismantled in an afternoon. The golf course was also open and unfenced, so whenever we had a hit, we were tagged by a posse of barefoot local kids.

Nathan and his wife, Martha, were standing awkwardly out the front of the clubhouse. When I'd first seen Nathan, I hadn't been able to take my eyes off him. The Bougainville people were renowned for having the blackest skin of all the islanders but until you saw it you couldn't appreciate just how blue-black it really was.

Dad strode towards them. 'I'm sorry to have kept you waiting. Trouble in the kitchen.' He grinned. 'Come on, let's get you good people a seat.'

He steered them gently towards the tables. Conversation

in the room went quiet as Dad escorted them through.

'Yoo-hoo,' Phyllis, the doctor's wife, shrieked from the nearest table. 'Come and join me. Sidney's working so I'm all alone.'

Dad took care of the introductions as we sat down. 'Have you met my deputy, Nathan?'

'No. We'll have to get him and his good lady involved in our comp, won't we?'

'Nathan's too busy to learn golf. He'll be DC soon.'

Phyllis looked stunned. 'But, Bill, where will that leave you?'

'Fishing somewhere, I hope.' Dad had a twinkle in his eye. 'Couple of my mates have moved to Coff's Harbour, and they reckon the fishing's brilliant there. Want me to join them in their charter business.'

'So, Phyllis, what exotic dish did you bring this time?' Mum asked.

'You'll never guess!' Phyllis' eyes flashed. 'Snails!'

'Bloody hell. Are we in Gay Paree?' Dad laughed.

'You *are* a joker, Bill. Apparently, the Japanese brought them here during the war. Our houseboy showed me how to clean and cook them.'

My mother wrinkled her nose but Dad grinned. 'I'm sure they'll be beaut with a bit of garlic butter.'

Phyllis turned to Nathan. 'You must be from Bougainville, young man.'

He nodded stiffly.

Phyllis turned to Dad. 'Weren't they from Bougainville, those two fellows who were set upon and killed in the Highlands? Such a dreadful thing to happen, especially after we'd gone to all that trouble to train them.'

Nathan spoke slowly, 'Payback is a terrible thing.'

'It was a tragedy, all right. This country won't survive long if you people keep killing each other like that!'

She flounced off in the direction of the food table. Nathan was looking at Martha. Her head was bowed and she was rubbing the tablecloth between her fingers.

'Perhaps I should take my wife home,' Nathan said to Dad. 'She finds social gatherings hard.'

Dad patted Martha's hand. 'You stand your ground, girl. Don't let them scare you.'

I thought she would flinch at the contact but instead a shy smile crept across her face, and from that point on, she gradually relaxed. We all worked to protect her from Phyllis' good intentions.

After the last of the desserts had been eaten, someone put some music on the PA and kids started dancing on the edge of the dance floor. When the old favourite 'Promised

Land' came on, Dad jumped up. 'Come on, girls, I love this one. You can't let me dance alone.'

Rosie and I stood but then he turned to the rest of the table. 'Girls …' He held out his hands.

Martha looked at Nathan and slowly moved forward. Phyllis and my mother were already out on the dance floor, and we all started swaying in a circle around my father.

Dad shouted back to the table. 'Come on, Nathan. Help me out, will you?'

Nathan shuffled out and he and Martha began to dance a stiff waltz together.

Rosie nudged me. 'They're dancing just like white people – total lack of rhythm.'

When the party broke up soon afterwards, Martha came forward and shook each of our hands shyly.

Back home, I waylaid Dad on his way to the bathroom.

'What was Phyllis saying about those men being killed in the Highlands? I haven't heard anything about it.'

Dad looked uncomfortable. 'They didn't report it in the news.'

'What happened?'

'Two Buka officers accidentally ran over a child. The mob pulled them from the station Land Rover and beat them to death.' He sighed. 'The worst of it was they were bloody good men. One of them was earmarked for the Health Ministry.' He lowered his voice. 'You can see why I don't want Nathan to get involved in the brawl out on the island. We can't afford to lose any more good local officers.'

'Daddy, *we* can't afford to lose *you* …'

'Enough of that kind of talk. Time for bed, my girl.'

The smorgasbord had been a welcome diversion but I woke the next morning in a tangle of emotions. There were two Errols: the one with the smart mouth and the hard eyes and the one who had laid his head in my lap, and I needed to know which one was the real Errol.

The best way to get in touch with him was through Desmond. My mother had heard on the Golf Club grapevine that Desmond was a 'Grammar' boy, so she didn't mind if I spent time with him. 'Just as a friend, of course, Billie. It wouldn't be fair to get his hopes up.'

So, next morning I walked to the Wu Trading Emporium. Desmond must have seen me coming because suddenly he was standing there in the doorway, gesturing me in. As I slid past his outstretched arm, I felt safe.

He turned his slow-burning smile in my direction. 'Can I help you, Billie?'

I sensed a hesitation, as though he was expecting me to ask for Errol, so I decided to bide my time. I'd spend half an hour or so with him and then casually ask about Errol.

'I'm bored at home. Can I hang out with you for a while?'

He smiled. 'I've got to keep an eye on the shop but we could listen to some music in the back room. I've got *Sticky Fingers*.'

He held up the cover with its oversized denim groin and we shared a blush. He led me through a beaded curtain with a picture of the Mona Lisa on it into a storeroom. Shelves lined the walls, packed with cans, bottles and packages. A small divan was squashed into the corner. The room was cool in the semi-darkness and the smell of sandalwood was comforting.

'My God, you've got so much stuff here. You're here for the long haul.'

'Not really. My parents talk about leaving when they think I'm not listening. We won't qualify for citizenship – rumour is you'll have to have at least one grandparent born here. They're afraid of getting chucked out at independence and losing everything.'

I nearly sat on a sketchbook as I settled on the divan. The top sketch was the trade store, detailed right down to the patterns on the hanging sarongs and the individual salty plums in the giant jars on the counter. In the artist's hands, the room had transformed into an Aladdin's cave of beauty and mystery.

'Did you do this?'

Desmond blushed his characteristic peach.

'It's amazing,' I said. 'Are there more?'

He laughed. 'I've got sketchbooks full but I keep them out of the way. My folks can't see the point of my scribbles, as they call them.'

I leafed through his drawings. There were landscapes of the town and the reefs, portraits, and intricate studies of everyday things, like a pair of toggles on Chinese pyjamas. They were all exquisite.

'You've got so much talent,' I said. 'What are you going to do next year?'

'My parents want me to do a business degree.'

'Not art?'

'Art doesn't lead to a proper job.'

He slipped the record on the turntable and the raw opening riff of 'Brown Sugar' filled the room. We grinned at each other and leant back against the wall, moving our feet with the music, mimicking Mick Jagger and laughing. Every so often the shop bell rang and Desmond jumped up and turned the volume down as he passed the record player.

A tiny old lady in silk pyjamas shuffled in. She spoke sharply and he followed her out a back door. When he came back he was smiling. 'My great-aunt. She was born in a little village in China and she still can't get the hang of taps.'

Around noon his cousin Shirley dropped by. I liked her straight away. She had an untidy perm that looked out of proportion to her tiny body and said things like 'You're kidding, Dessie' as she shoved him in the ribs.

To make room for her on the divan, I had to shift closer to Desmond until our thighs were touching. Shirley's teasing way was catching and I found myself nuzzling under his shoulder. 'I wish you were *my* cousin, Desmond.'

A shadow passed across his face.

'I better go home,' I said. 'I'm dreading it though – another argument with my mother.'

'About what?'

'She wants me to go to Vanessa's party this weekend – I can't think of anything worse. None of my real friends will be there – you're not going, are you?'

He laughed and shook his head. When he spoke, his voice was silky. 'If your mother wants you to go, you should go.' He looked directly into my eyes before he continued,

'Besides, if you don't go, *she* will know why and you can't give her the satisfaction.'

He was talking about Vanessa. We looked at each other for what felt like ages as an understanding passed between us. I had to pull my gaze away.

It was only as I began to skip down the road that it occurred to me that I'd completely forgotten Errol.

# Chapter 13

## A Clockwork Orange

A car horn interrupted my thoughts. Lucille's Mini Moke had pulled off the road just in front of me. She wore a red and white sailor dress, white sunglasses and a wide grin.

'Hey, kiddo, you been out of town?'

'I went down to Keriva with my dad.'

'So, I guess you saw Errol? Get in, honey.' She gestured across to the front seat. 'He wants you to go to the movies at the Imperial tonight,' she said, when I was seated.

'I don't know, Lucille. He was kind of mean out there.'

She squeezed my arm. 'He really likes you, I can tell. And Vanessa's been parading around town with some white guy. Promise me you'll come tonight.'

'How come you care so much?'

She looked wistful. 'The happiest time of my life was when I was your age. Everything was such an adventure. I want to help you enjoy it as much as you can.'

Hearing her say she envied my youth was strange – I envied her experience, her coolness, her … everything.

'Can you help me get around my parents then?'

'Don't worry. I'll give you a lift home and I'll ask your mother if you can come out with me tonight. She likes me, doesn't she?'

'Doesn't everyone?'

But Mum started in on me as soon as the door opened.

'Where have you been, young lady? Madeleine Barry was on the telephone about Vanessa's party and I couldn't find you.'

I stepped back so she could see Lucille. 'I've been at Desmond's. Look who I bumped into on the way home.'

'Lucille, always a pleasure.'

'I dropped in to ask if Billie could come to the movies with me tonight.'

'She's been out quite a lot lately.'

'It's the holidays, though, isn't it?' Lucille laughed.

Mum's lips were tight. 'I think it's our business when Billie goes out.'

I squirmed at my mother's rudeness.

'What film is it?' Mum asked.

'It's called *A Clockwork Orange*. I think it's some kind of musical.'

'Please, Mum.'

'Well, if it's a musical, I suppose there's no harm …'

She began to interrogate me as soon as Lucille had left. 'Where were you again?'

'I told you, with Desmond. You know, the Grammar boy?'

'I hear he comes from quite a good family, as they go … but really, Billie. Don't you wonder how they can live in those little fibro boxes? Their money seems wasted on them.'

I wasn't going to let her get away with that. 'Actually, he happens to agree with you about Vanessa's party.'

I was enjoying the confusion on her face. 'I'm not sure I understand.'

'Desmond thinks I should go to the party to make you happy. I told you he was a nice boy.'

'Well, that's settled then.' Mum smiled triumphantly. 'I told Madeleine you'd be going – and now I have it from the horse's mouth.'

As Lucille drove to the Imperial, I looked out into the dark and thought about Errol. Used to be when Vanessa clicked her fingers, he jumped. Now there was a chance it was me he wanted. There was a low pulse of excitement in my belly as we parked.

The first time I had gone to the Imperial had been an adventure. This time it looked tatty under the fluorescents. Dark faces peered at us, and I recalled my fear of the silent crowd closing in around us on the island.

Lucille sat down in a row of chairs just inside the doors. They were upright and uncomfortable with hard metal bars between them. Lucille had moved three seats in so there was a free one left on the end, next to me. I sat chewing Fantales, nervous about Errol's arrival but more nervous that he wouldn't come.

'Hello, Billie. Is this seat free?'

It was Desmond, sweet Desmond blundering into Lucille's best-laid plan.

'For you, Desmond, of course.'

He looked different somehow, like he'd made an effort. His hair had grown longer over the holidays and was brushed so it ran like silk to his shoulders.

'Desmond? What are you doing here, baby?' Lucille asked.

'Oh, you're keeping a seat for him, I get it …'

Lucille stood and pushed past me and Desmond as she moved out into the aisle. 'Take mine.'

'Please.' I stood to let him in.

'You two look cosy.' Errol slid into the empty seat at the end. He leant across and caught the neckline of Desmond's shirt in his hands. It was a sheer caftan top, a delicate shade of ivory that was almost pink.

'Where d'you get this thing from? You look like a ponce.'

'Shirley brought it back from Rabaul.' Desmond turned to me. 'She gave it to me after you left today.'

'You two been together today?'

'I hung out at his place for a while. You're wrong about the shirt.' I turned to Desmond. 'It looks great on you.'

Errol leant over and took my hand. He squeezed it so tightly I gasped, just as the lights went out.

The camera opened on the face of the main character, Alex, made up with false eyelashes and white powder like a crazy clown. Then it panned out and he was sitting in a bar, surrounded by white plastic mannequins of naked women kneeling on all fours. Their breasts were huge and their nipples leered forward. God, I thought, what have I got myself into?

The film was probably the worst I could have seen with a boy I wanted sitting on one side and a boy I respected sitting on the other. The violence and sex made me squirm. I'd never seen anyone naked on the screen before and suddenly Alex was cutting a woman's clothes off, revealing pink nipples above milky breasts.

The rape scene was frightening but I couldn't look away. I felt ashamed and yet transfixed. It was like they were my pink nipples up there on the screen for everyone to see.

The local crowd was treating it like a comedy, laughing as the gang kicked an old man, and hooting in the clothes-cutting scene. To them it was a pantomime, with a few tits and bums thrown in.

I became aware of the boys' thighs pressing against mine through the metal bars on each side. Errol still had hold of my hand when the lights went down but as the images began to unfold on the screen, he loosened his grip, until only our fingertips were touching. As the rape scene started his fingers slipped away, leaving my hand alone on the armrest. I didn't dare look at him, but I imagined him wearing his stony look.

I felt equally awkward about Desmond on the other side. Would he have closed his eyes when he caught a glimpse of that pinkness? Was he holding his breath like me? Was he sharing my discomfort, my shame? I tightened my thighs to try to minimise the contact that I felt in the gap under the armrests. I wanted to stand up, to walk out, but I was frozen.

A hissing from behind broke the spell. Lucille was gesturing for us to follow her.

Once we were outside, she let loose, 'Sorry, but I had to get you out of there, Billie. No way is that a movie for a young lady! What kind of sick person makes a movie like that, anyway?'

She sounded surprisingly like my mother but I didn't care – I was so grateful to have been rescued. The boys shuffled awkwardly.

'Come back to my place,' Lucille said. 'I'll tell Billie's mother we left early, but we wanted to make sure she was okay before we took her home.'

Errol and I nodded our agreement, but Desmond hung back in the shadows as if he wasn't sure what to do. I felt safe with him around but more than anything I wanted to be alone with Errol.

'I better get back,' Desmond said. 'Shirley is still in there.'

'Okay …'

The others had already turned and were moving towards the Mini Moke. I watched Desmond walk away, the muscles in his back rising and falling under the thin fabric like a shadow play. I felt as I had the first time I'd met him on this very spot, like I'd offended him but wasn't sure how.

When we got to Lucille's, she disappeared inside to fix some drinks, leaving Errol and me alone on the verandah. The harbour lights shimmering through the trees drew me forward into the dark and he followed.

I turned to face him. 'You've got a cheek, asking me to the movies after you were so mean yesterday.'

'Mean? I thought your father was going to punch me.'

'You went out of your way to provoke him, talking about me like that.'

'I lost my temper, I admit. I thought we might finally get to run our own country. But Don's still calling the tune and your dad's still his monkey.'

'Dad's nothing like Don. If you don't know that, you don't understand us at all.'

Errol leant forward and pushed back a strand of hair that had fallen across my eyes. 'You're a big girl, Billie. You don't have to side with Daddy. It's time to make up your own mind.'

He took a step closer and his body locked into place with mine as though it was meant to be. I'd been waiting for this since I took him to the bunker, playing the scene over and over again in my head.

He lifted me into the fork of a frangipani tree and jammed his body hard up against mine so I couldn't move. The force winded me.

'Errol, come out, come out wherever you are,' Lucille called from the verandah in a tipsy voice. 'I promised Billie's mum I'd look after her.'

Errol slid me back down to the ground and we moved into the light. 'We were just enjoying the view.'

'Do me a favour, I was young once too, you know. Time I took Billie home.'

'Haven't you had a few drinks, cuz? I'll run her home. Her old man won't see me if I park under the tree.'

I sat staring out at the darkness as Errol reversed down the driveway and turned back along the coast road. His force had taken me by surprise, frightened me even, but maybe that was what passion looked like?

'I need to show you something,' he said.

He turned the car in the opposite direction to my house and my stomach fell. 'Where are you taking me?'

'To my island, of course.'

'What, tonight? Are you crazy? Stop the car, stop it right now.'

For a few seconds, I wasn't sure whether he'd do as I asked or not. Images of him pushing me up against the tree, sniggering with the boys on the island, and sneering at my father flashed into my mind.

He braked and the car jerked to a halt. 'Calm down, Billie.'

'I can't just nick off in the middle of the night.'

'I thought you were brave.'

'But I'm not stupid. They'd miss me and we'd both be in a lot of trouble. I'm not supposed to even see you.'

He was silent for a few moments. 'Okay. But promise you'll come tomorrow morning?'

I nodded.

He let me out a couple of houses up from ours. 'Pick you up around nine?'

'Okay. Dad will be well gone by then.'

My father was slumped in his armchair when I walked in.

He rubbed his eyes. 'Are you back already?'

'It was such an awful film we walked out and went back to Lucille's place.'

'I hope you weren't tempted to touch any liquor.'

'Not me.' I breathed theatrically in his direction. It was an effort to try to look demure, as I remembered the pressure of Errol against my jeans.

Dad rolled his eyes. 'Butter wouldn't melt, hey?'

# Chapter 14

## Shark calling

There were butterflies in my stomach next morning as I slipped down to the coast road. The VW Fastback was waiting under a tree. Errol leant across and opened the passenger door. He was wearing rugby shorts and his shark's tooth. He shot me a sideways glance that did nothing to ease my nerves.

The windows were open and the wind noise would have made conversation difficult even if I'd wanted to talk. Which I didn't. The boy driving the car was the angry Errol so there wasn't any point.

As we sped south down the coast road, the rows of coconut trees went by faster and faster until the separate trunks blended into one. Every now and then there was a gap – a clearing, a shed, a house – which interrupted the rhythm of the road, and then I lapsed back into it again.

Eventually the car slowed and turned into a dirt road. We bumped along for a few minutes until the Barry copra shed appeared ahead.

'That's quicker than the boat,' I said.

Errol jumped out and strode ahead of me down to the beach. He dragged a speedboat into the water and held its bow still so I could step into it. The outboard motor screamed into action as we powered towards the island.

Instead of heading for the jetty, Errol steered towards the ocean side of the island. We rounded the headland and he dropped the engine right down so he could pick a path over the reef that ran along that side of the island. Once the coral had given way to sand, he killed the engine and jumped into the shallows. The water splashed up from his thighs as he dragged the boat towards the shore. He leant across me as he pulled it onto the beach and a drip of seawater made me shiver.

'There's my place.' Errol guided me towards the hut under the trees with the gentle pressure of two fingers in the middle of my back.

I pushed open the woven door and looked inside. It was dark and cool and there was a close smell that was somehow comforting. In the corner was a makeshift desk, an old door on a pair of builder's horses. There was a pile of books on it and I recognised some of the names on the spines – Marx, Malcolm X, Che Guevara.

'Not a bad library, is it? If you read some of this stuff, you'd understand what I'm on about.' He picked up a volume. 'This is the first published book by a Papua New Guinean. It's called *The Crocodile*. Bet your dad doesn't know we can write books, hey?'

My eyes rested on the single bed against the far wall. I felt a thrill in the pit of my stomach, tinged with fear. The only sounds were the lapping of the waves on the sand and my heart thumping in my chest. I remembered Errol's strength from the night before. Now he was standing right behind me, a little too close, and nobody even knew I was there.

I stepped around him and out into the sunlight. 'I thought you lived with your mother?'

'She lives behind the store, and I don't want anything to do with that place anymore. Nobody bothers me over here and I'm free to go out calling sharks whenever I feel like it.'

'Shark calling? I thought they only did that on Tabar Island.'

He laughed. 'Where do you think Tabar Island is? Just a bit further out there.' He pointed out to sea. 'Mum's father came from Tabar.'

'Did he teach you?'

'He was long dead when I came along. Thank God. He wouldn't have approved of Cedric. But he gave me the shark caller's spirit.'

'What exactly is shark calling?'

He walked across to a canoe on the sand, reached in and picked up a rattle made from pieces of coconut shell.

'You sit in your canoe and call on the shark spirits. Then you bang this on the water until one comes, and when he does, you slip a noose made of vines around his neck. Nothing to it.'

'Isn't it dangerous?'

'Only if you don't know how to finish them off.' He lifted a wooden club up out of the canoe.

'What's this for then?' I reached into the canoe and held up a knife. The outline of a shark tooth was scratched into it.

'That's to cut the shark up afterwards. Careful, the blade's sharp.' He leant across and carefully took it from me.

'Do you really believe you can call the shark spirits?'

He narrowed his eyes. 'Do you think I'm a fake, Billie? Because I read books and know how to put my words together, you think I don't believe in spirits?'

I blushed.

'Oh, I believe in spirits all right. That's why I need to

show you this. Come on.' He turned and began striding along a track into the bush.

I followed, flinching as the kunai grass slashed my thighs. After a few minutes, Errol stopped at a scruffy-looking bush and pushed part of the vegetation aside to reveal a hidden path.

This path led to a clearing and in the centre stood a new hut, about five feet off the ground with a bamboo ladder up to the tiny entrance. It wasn't built for men but for the child-sized *malangan* statues I saw in the shadows within.

Something was scratching underneath. I leant down and saw a small man hunched over. It looked like Tobias but his face was twisted away. He was holding a feather and something white and crumpled and wrapping them tightly together. He chanted as he worked, regular as breathing.

Our ghost stories rely on darkness, on things going bump in the night. But the sight of the little man scratching under the spirit house on a day so bright it hurt my eyes chilled me.

Errol called out, 'What are you doing?'

His voice should have startled the old man, but Tobias turned his head like he was in a dream.

'I said, what are you doing, old man? Does the kiap know you've built your own spirit house? Because his daughter's going to tell him.'

As Tobias turned his slow gaze on me, I felt a prick of fear at the back of my neck.

'Stop it, Errol,' I pleaded.

He kept going, 'You know his daughter, don't you, Tobias? She's my friend.'

Tobias' hooded eyes were like cowrie shells. 'Meri i tambu.' Women are forbidden.

He dropped his head and resumed chanting.

Errol took my hand and led me back onto the main path. I was too frightened to speak until we were out of sight of the old man.

'You shouldn't have provoked him like that.'

'You're right to be scared of him. He's a sangguma. Do you know what that is?'

I'd heard the word whispered since I was a child, and I knew enough to be afraid of it. 'Some kind of magic man?'

'One who'll do *anything* to get what they want.'

'Shouldn't we get out of here then?'

Errol laughed. 'You're safe as long as you're with me. My friends will protect us. It's your father you should worry about.'

'My father knows what he's doing.'

'He thinks Tobias is his friend. You have to convince him he's not.'

'We're not close like we used to be.' It was the first time I'd admitted it, and it hurt.

But Errol wasn't listening. 'Come meet my mother.'

It was only about a fifteen-minute walk from the spirit house to the village, but the sweat was dripping down my back by the time we walked out of the bush. A few young guys lounging under the trees called out and whistled but they shut up when Errol looked at them.

He led me to a small shed; a window was propped open by two wooden stakes to reveal a counter. The woman standing behind it had Errol's soft eyes and full lips. When she saw him, it was like a light had been switched on inside her. Her hair, plaited and wrapped around her head, shone out like a grey halo and her skin tightened with joy.

'Mum, this is Billie.'

We stood awkwardly, not sure how to approach each other. I held out my hand and she reached for the other one as well.

'Pleased to meet you, Miss Billie. I'm May.'

'Call me Billie. Please.'

'Okay, *Billie*. What are you doing down here without the masta?'

'I brought her down,' Errol said. 'I wanted to show her what Tobias has been up to. So she can go home and tell her father.'

She nodded. 'Tobias always been against my family. He no like my father because he come from Tabar, and now he no like my boy. He crazy jealous. Errol got brains. Tobias, well Tobias is … long long.' She tapped her head.

'I'd better take Billie home before they miss her, Mum.'

As soon as we walked back into the bush, Errol's words burst out, 'She shouldn't have gone into all that family history. You can't be expected to understand island politics.'

'Try me.'

'Tobias doesn't like me because I'm half-caste. The old way was that you do anything for a wantok, someone from your tribe … but to Tobias and his cronies I'm an outsider, I'll never be their wantok.'

'But the young people are different?'

'They know I can deal with white men. I've lived in their world.'

The sun was strong and my head felt fuzzy. I hadn't had anything since breakfast. An insect buzz rose from the bush but above that a strange slapping noise seemed to ricochet around. Errol held his hand up and we stopped dead. A shout rang out before more rhythmic slapping. The sound was coming from off to the side, and I realised that we were back at the turnoff near the spirit house. Errol lifted the curtain of vines and we edged along the track until we were close enough to make out figures without them seeing us.

About half a dozen old men were standing in line at the far end of the clearing. They wore dark *lap-laps* and had some kind of sash across their upper body. Wooden guns were hoisted over their shoulders and they appeared to be drilling like soldiers.

Tobias was standing in front of them, wearing his *luluai* cap, with a scrap of something white tied around it like a hat band.

'Attention,' Tobias called.

The troop came to attention with a slap of arms and thighs.

'Yes, Masta DC,' they shouted.

Errol raised his eyebrows and I realised he'd heard it as well.

Tobias dismissed the troop and we watched silently as the old soldiers departed. He took off his cap and turned it over in his hands as he began to chant again. It struck me that this piece of white cloth was probably the one we'd seen him chanting over earlier.

We slipped back into the bush and walked back to the speedboat. Errol seemed preoccupied and a silence sat between us as we returned to the mainland.

Once we were sitting in his car, he grabbed my hand and squeezed so tight I winced. 'You heard them. *Masta* DC, they said. As clear as day. He wants to replace your father. You've got to get home and warn him about the sangguma.'

*Sangguma.* The word echoed inside my head until it became the rhythm of the road the whole way home.

# Chapter 15

## Soul music

As the front door banged behind me, Mum came barrelling out of the kitchen. 'Where have you been? I've been worried sick.'

'I need to talk to Dad.'

'He'll be home soon.'

'I can't wait that long. I'm going down to the office.'

I was out the back door before she had time to open her mouth.

The line of wooden offices was set back from the road behind a triangle of manicured grass. Nathan was standing in Dad's office when I rushed in. They looked like they were in the middle of something.

'Steady on, Billie,' Dad said. 'Haven't you heard of knocking?'

'I need to talk to you.'

'Shoot.'

I glanced at Nathan. 'It's kind of personal.'

'If it's about that boy down on Keriva, don't worry, we were just talking about him.'

I blushed. 'I've just come back from the island. Errol showed me something really important.'

'I thought I told you not to see him anymore.'

'Dad, Tobias has already built that spirit house he doesn't want you to know about. In the middle of the island.'

'That's not a crime, is it?'

'There's something else.'

I hesitated, realising how hard it was to convey how sinister the strange rituals had been. 'Errol told me to tell you Tobias is a … sangguma.'

Dad grinned at Nathan. 'Goodness, a sangguma. Whatever shall we do?'

'They were doing some strange marching drill. And Tobias was pretending to be you. They called him Masta DC.'

'I think we need a beer to help us digest *that* news. Don't you agree, Nathan?'

I followed them out to a gravel carpark. They got into the front of a khaki Land Rover and I climbed into the back. Dad was fond of the old jeeps but he'd never had to bounce up and down on their metal seats.

Back home, Dad settled Nathan on the back verandah. 'Billie, get us a couple of cold ones, would you?'

As I came back with the tray, Dad said, 'Those pricks in Moresby wouldn't know if their arse was on fire.'

'You can't ignore what they said. About encouraging the lad.'

'Over my dead body, mate. I understand you might have to work with him in the future but fair dinkum – feeding my daughter that crap about Tobias being the boogie man ...'

As I went back into the kitchen, I heard Nathan say, 'I'm going down there first thing Monday.'

Nathan left after he'd finished his drink and I took another one out to Dad. His face was set in a hard line. 'I told you to stay away from that boy.'

'Don't you get it, Dad? They were calling him "Masta DC", like he plans to replace you.'

'You're seriously warning me about a bunch of old men?'

'It was really scary, Dad.'

'That smug bastard has you eating out of his hand. Can't you see he's using you to get to me?'

'Because he couldn't possibly be interested in me just for myself?'

'You're a child, Billie.' He grabbed my arm. 'He hasn't tried anything on with you, has he?'

'No. But we may as well, you're going to think it anyway.'

I was so angry that I stormed down the steps and was away before I'd even thought about it. The trip to Keriva and the rush back to warn my father had been a total waste of time. Maybe Dad would've listened to me if I'd been a boy. Instead, he'd been blinded by his prejudice; his fear that a black man might get his hands on his little girl.

Errol had mentioned something about Desmond's when he'd dropped me off so I walked along the road to Chinatown. It was getting dark and I was relieved to see the Fastback parked out the front of Wu's Emporium.

There was a closed sign on the door and it was locked when I turned the knob. I was trying to figure out whether any of the buildings nearby might be Desmond's home when the door swung open.

Desmond looked surprised. 'Billie, what are you doing here? It's late ...'

'I had a fight with my dad. Is Errol here?'

He led me out to the back room. Record covers were strewn across the floor and a man's voice was rising and falling hypnotically from the speakers in the corner. Errol was leaning back on the divan but he stood and moved forward to greet me. I could sense Desmond hovering behind me.

'I tried to tell Dad about what we saw today but he wouldn't listen. I don't know what to do ...'

'Your timing's perfect. Desmond's playing his new Marvin Gaye.'

'Do you like soul music?' Desmond asked.

I shrugged, not wanting to admit I'd never really listened to it before. Errol moved into the space in front of me. 'You don't just listen to this music. You've got to feel it. In here ...' His hands rested on each of my hipbones and a tingle ran between them. 'And in here.' One hand slid up to rest on my breastbone. I blushed, feeling Desmond's eyes on us.

'Maybe you'd prefer the Four Tops. This is one of my favourites.' Desmond bent over the turntable and suddenly the music was pulling me in. My foot tapped to the rhythm and as the voices started a wave of emotion carried me up somewhere I'd never been before.

Then the words started to register. It was all about helpless love. Was Desmond mocking me? He was still fumbling around near the record player so I couldn't see his face.

'Was that the door?' Errol asked.

Desmond lifted the needle, and I heard the knock and an old woman's voice.

Desmond smiled. 'That'll be aunty, calling me to dinner. I better go tell her I've got company.'

He shot a kind of warning look at Errol before he turned on his heel and left. A feeling of unfinished business hung in the air.

Errol moved across to the record player and bumped off the Four Tops. Marvin Gaye started murmuring again and Errol began to move against me. It wasn't so much dancing as graceful staggering as his hands moved over my body. He kissed me hard and I fell back against the divan.

I was about to protest when he reached down and popped open the button on my shorts. I knew it was crazy but I couldn't think about anything but what his fingers were doing. Don't stop, I thought, please don't stop.

The swish of the curtain made Errol jump up.

'We need to talk,' Desmond said.

I stayed on the divan with my eyes closed as they went back into the shop. There were some muffled angry exchanges and then the front door banged.

I knew I should get up but I felt winded. When Desmond walked back in, it was all I could do to roll on to my side and try to pull the two edges of my zipper together to cover my bare belly.

'What was that about?' I whispered.

He squatted down and carefully laid an envelope on the divan next to me. 'This was on the floor of the shop. It must have fallen out of his pocket.'

I read the name scrawled on the front. *Vanessa.*

'I've watched him do it to so many girls. But this time it's different. This time it's you.'

'But Lucille said it was over.'

'He tries to forget her but he just can't. I think Lucille really thought you might be the answer. She didn't mean you to get hurt – but family is everything to her.'

Family. I had a fleeting feeling of guilt about running out on my father. Dragging myself to a seated position, I held my gaping shorts together.

'Let's get you fixed up, hey.' Desmond took me gently by the shoulders and lifted me up to standing. Then he reached down and ever so carefully pulled my shorts together and fastened the button. We both held our breath as he slid the zipper up.

The plastic curtain rattled to reveal Shirley. She was

grinning as though a funny story was bubbling on her lips but the grin disappeared when she saw us. Rather than trying to explain, I whisked the envelope up and slid it into my back pocket.

'I need to take Billie home,' Desmond said.

I followed him into a garage the size of a small aircraft hangar, where a polished cream Mercedes with red leather seats was parked.

'Your parents'?'

He nodded.

I blushed. 'I've never even met them.'

'They spend most of their time in the bakery.'

The smell of the upholstery was exotic but comforting, like pipe tobacco. I shut my eyes and kept them squeezed tight until the car stopped. When I opened them, Desmond was looking across at me.

'I'm sorry if I've come between you and Errol,' I said.

'It was bound to happen.'

'I feel like such a fool ...'

Desmond shrugged. 'It's hard to resist that killer charm of his. And he's so ambitious. Sooner or later he'll abandon all his friends.'

'Even her?'

'They're taking a hell of a risk already. What are you going to do with the letter?'

'I'm not sure.'

'Well, don't leave it lying around. It could get them in a lot of trouble.'

We sat quietly for a couple of minutes.

I looked up at the house. 'I should go in. But I'm afraid ...'

He rubbed my hand. 'You can do it, Billie. Just get through Vanessa's party and I'll be right here when you get back.'

'What did I ever do to deserve a friend like you?'

I kissed him just once as I got out of the car. I was aiming for his cheek but somehow our lips touched, and as they pulled apart I felt a little charge.

I made myself walk to the bottom of our front steps before I turned around. He was still there, parked under a tree in the dark. He raised his arm as the Mercedes slowly moved off.

# Chapter 16

## A toad in a safari suit

I was relieved that Tahl greeted me at the front door, but as he led me towards the dining room and I heard a strange voice, I realised we had company. I walked in hesitantly, checking my face in the mirror and pulling down the hem of my shorts. My stomach lurched when I saw Cedric Chan – short and overblown like a toad in a safari suit – sitting between my parents.

'I don't think you've met our local member of parliament, Mr Chan?' Mum said. 'This is our youngest, Billie.'

'Delighted.'

The only resemblance between Errol and the flat, inexpressive face in front of me were the heavy eyes. But while Errol's drew you in, Cedric's shut you out.

'I understand you know my nephew. I've been trying to explain to your father how important Errol will be to the future of this country. He's a natural leader.'

'The boy's a charmer, all right, but I'm not sure I trust him,' Dad said.

'I think you'll find your superiors disagree. And you'd be very foolish to get in his way.' Cedric fixed his eyes on me. 'Talk some sense into your father.'

Dad stood without offering his hand. 'Tahl, show Mr Chan the door.'

They'd barely left the room when Dad exploded, 'That sounded like a bloody threat to me. He's nothing but a jumped-up trade store owner but he acts like he's got a hotline to the Chief Minister.'

'Come on, let's go finish our dinner. Honestly, I thought the man'd never leave.' As Mum began steering Dad towards the kitchen, she turned back to me. 'You'd better join us, Billie. You can't miss *another* meal.'

'Where the hell have you been, anyway?' Dad asked.

Rosie grinned across from where she sat, the remains of her meal in front of her. She was enjoying the fact that I was getting in trouble for a change.

'I had to tell Errol you're ignoring his warning about Tobias.'

Dad spluttered across the table, 'So, he got his father to come and threaten me. What more do I have to do to convince you the boy's bad news?'

'Funnily enough, he's done that himself.'

'I don't want you walking the streets after dark,' Mum said.

'Desmond drove me home. I didn't feel well … I don't think I'll be able to go tomorrow.'

'You'll be at that party if I have to drag you there myself,' Mum said.

'Susan doesn't have to go to the stupid party.'

'Susan's got a very responsible job down at the nuns'. If you were doing something worthwhile like that …'

Story of my life. Susan's the clever one, Rosie's the pretty one and Billie … well, Billie's the odd one out.

As soon as I could I headed for the safety of my room, but Rosie followed me. 'Gosh, that Cedric Chan's a creep. Beats me how you can be interested in his nephew.'

'Didn't you hear what I told Dad?'

'I thought you were just saying that so you can sneak off and shag him.'

I turned to push her away and the envelope fell onto the floor.

Rosie looked down. 'What's that?'

It had fallen with the name facing upwards. I picked it up and jammed it back into my pocket, but Rosie had already read it.

'Vanessa? I thought you hated Vanessa?'

I shrugged, desperately trying to think of a cover story.

Rosie smirked. 'But it's not your writing, is it, little sister? You're running a message for someone.'

She looked thoughtful. 'That would explain why Vanessa's been so cool about her new boyfriend, Angus. He flew over to spend the week with her before her birthday party.'

'So?'

'The day he arrived, she disappeared and I had to look after him. I'd *never* leave a boy like that with a girl like me.'

'So, did you steal him away?'

'Don't try and change the subject. You may as well come clean, you know I'm just going to keep pestering until you do.'

'Actually, Karl asked me to give it to her.' The lie came to me fully formed.

'Who the hell is Karl?'

'Max's son. You know, the one who used to wear long socks and sandals to Sunday school. I saw him at the wharf the other day and he asked me to give it to her. Didn't seem any harm in it.'

'He hasn't got a chance.'

I pushed my door open. 'I better start packing or Mum'll kill me.'

Safely inside, I leant back against the door and took the envelope out. I was used to letters written on delicate pale-blue aerograms, but this one was thick and smudged. Only my pride stopped me ripping it open; instead, I shoved it into my toilet bag.

I wasn't sure whether I wanted to give the letter to Vanessa or not, but holding it made me feel I had some power over her. Maybe I could at least keep a bit of my pride.

I swung open my cupboard door and looked at the meagre offerings inside. My mother would insist on a dress for the party, and I only owned two. It would have to be the white seersucker with red spots. It was the kind of no-frills dress a ten year old might wear, the only kind I could tolerate. The one I'd worn to the Imperial that first night with Errol back when I thought I was on the brink of a great adventure and didn't know Vanessa existed. A lifetime ago.

Dropping my shorts, I looked down where his hands had been barely an hour ago. The dress was a little tight across my back, so I undid the zipper enough to ease off Susan's padded bra and tossed it across the floor. Now the dress fitted snug and sexy. I could face Vanessa in this dress.

'Please tell me you're not wearing that to the party.' My mother had come in without me hearing and she was staring at me with her hands on her hips.

'What's the matter with it?'

'It draws attention to your bust, dear. I hate to say it, but it's not your best asset.'

'Well, I'm wearing it, so bad luck.'

Mum *tsked*. 'Let's hope Vanessa shows you how a young lady *should* behave.'

# Chapter 17

## Bad dream

A mosquito buzzed around my room as I checked the alarm clock once more. An hour since I went to bed and sleep seemed more out of reach than ever. I was running every moment in Desmond's storeroom back through my head, picking at my feelings like a scab. When Errol thrust against me, was he thinking of Vanessa's sweet skin? Had he ever cared about me, or had I just been a way to get at my father? And why did I feel guilty when I thought of Desmond? The mosquito circled round and round and the buzz moved in and out.

As I drifted off, the buzzing was inside my head and my nostrils filled with the stench of animal fat and mouldy wood. Wherever I was felt tight like a coffin, but I was standing on my feet. As my eyes adjusted, I could just make out wooden bars in front of my face. I grasped them and they were smooth, as though hundreds of hands had grasped them before me.

My scalp prickled with fear as I sensed a presence beside me. I knew without looking it was a *malangan*. Something sticky like a web touched my face and I jerked back.

I heard my father's voice, strong but muffled, and his shadowy outline loomed. He was looking at me but through me, as though I wasn't there.

Desperate for him to free me, I banged my fists on the bars, but they bounced off like they were made of rubber. I tried to scream but there was no sound.

My father paused under a ball of feathers swinging above the doorway and turned back in my direction. I thought at last he'd heard me, but he'd only turned to climb down a rickety-looking ladder. The top of that ladder looked familiar and then it hit me – I was stuck in the spirit house as my father began walking away into the light.

I was gripped by an even stronger panic when I saw a short shadow in front of him. Someone was leading him up the path away from me, and I suddenly realised the danger wasn't here in the dark but out there in the sunlight. I tried to scream but my legs gave way and I fell back into the darkness.

I jerked awake, heart pounding and struggling to breathe. Rolling over, my heartbeat and breathing slowed and I began to be conscious of voices, whispering insistently somewhere down the hall.

I looked at the face of the alarm clock. 12:15. My parents were never up this late. The panic of the dream propelled me down the hall towards their voices, which were coming from the kitchen.

'I simply can't believe it,' Mum said.

'My source was definite.'

A floorboard creaked so I pushed the door open. My parents sat at the kitchen table, looking guilty.

'What are *you* doing up?' Dad said.

I slumped down onto a chair. 'I had a bad dream. I was stuck inside the spirit house and a little man – Tobias, I think – was going to hurt you and I couldn't stop him. When I tried to scream no sound came out. It was so real, Daddy.' I felt tears dripping down my cheeks.

'It's okay, girl.' He reached into his pocket. 'Where's that damned handkerchief when I need it? Could have sworn I left it in these strides.'

'Why are you up so late? Has something happened?'

His nostrils flared. 'If you must know, that boy's been up to no good again.'

'Which boy? Errol?'

He nodded.

'What do you mean up to no good?'

He shook his head. 'I can't talk about it.'

He looked at me with his piercing eyes and my cheeks burnt with shame. He couldn't know what had happened in the storeroom, could he?

'When are the girls heading down to the Barrys?' Dad asked.

'Julius is taking them down after lunch,' Mum said.

'I'm going back to bed.' I slipped out and went quietly back to my bedroom, hoping my night light would ward off any more bad dreams.

I woke to the thud of movement down the hall and the hiss of an iron somewhere. My stomach growled with hunger and hot sunshine flooded the room; I must have slept in. The sheet was sticking to my legs, and I knew I should get up, but my mind was pulling me back into the suffocating fear of the dream and the strange scratching under the spirit house that had foreshadowed it.

There was a sharp rap on the door and Mum bustled in. 'Heavens, Billie, it's nearly time to leave and you haven't finished your packing, have you?'

'Mum, I really can't go …'

'Of course you're going. Not everyone was lucky enough to be invited, you know.' She picked up my dress from the back of my chair. 'Much as I hate this frock, you are going to put it on, you are going to look like a young lady in it and you are going to Vanessa's party.'

'Bathroom's free,' Rosie called out.

Mum nodded towards the door. 'Off you go then. When you're dressed, go into the kitchen and Tahl will make you a sandwich.'

The bathroom was a sanctuary with its cool water, smooth porcelain and shadowy corners. I stood under the shower until Rosie started banging on the door. As soon as I ventured out into the hallway, I heard her shouting for me to hurry.

In the kitchen, Dad and Tahl seemed to be sharing a silent communion as the household flurry went on outside.

Rosie barged in. 'The car's here.'

'There's still time to grab a bite before we hit the road,' Dad said.

'What do you mean *we*?'

'I thought I'd give Julius the day off – it is Saturday, after all. I'll drive you down and catch up with Don and Madeleine, might even stay the night.'

'Why would you want to do that?'

'Can't a man spend time with his girls without getting the third degree?' Dad was grinning but he wouldn't meet my eye.

Mum stood at the front door to see us off.

'Did you know Dad was planning to take us down?' My voice came out angrier than I meant.

'As a matter of fact, we did discuss it last night – not that it's any of your concern.'

'But don't you realise he's just using it as an excuse?'

'An excuse for what?'

'I bet he's going over to the island again – only this time he'll be alone.'

'Calm yourself, girl,' Dad said. 'Who said anything about going alone?'

'I just assumed …'

He grinned. 'Well, don't assume, okay? We'll pick up the excellent Sergeant on the way. You trust *him*, don't you?'

'Yes …' I turned to my mother. 'Please make him take more police, Mum.'

It was the first time in my life I'd asked my mother for help. We'd never had that kind of thing between us. That time I'd stood on a sea urchin as a child, it was Dad I'd called out for and who'd held me so tight while over his shoulder I saw Mum running for the first aid kit.

Mum tucked a stray hair into her bun. 'We have to trust your father on this one.'

'*You* used to trust my judgement, Billie.' Dad's eyes were sad and just for a moment I wanted to say I was sorry, but then I remembered how he'd ignored every single piece of help I'd tried to give him.

# Chapter 18

## The plantation

The trip down seemed interminable. Rosie chattered on and on as my nerves drew tighter. It was a relief when the white building finally loomed ahead.

Our old Statesman wound its awkward way up the driveway and halted beside a chipped concrete fountain.

'This place is so huge, isn't it?' I whispered.

'Try not to gawk,' Rosie said with a smirk.

Sergeant Eugene remained stiff in the front passenger seat. He'd looked uncomfortable throughout the trip down, staring ahead and resisting Dad's efforts to draw him into our conversation. But when Dad strode towards the entrance, Eugene was a few respectful steps behind.

Dad paused by the wide stone steps for us to catch up. 'Don't let that Vanessa lead you astray,' he muttered.

'What do you mean by that?' Rosie bristled.

'Just something I heard.' Dad caught my eye and I had the strangest feeling he knew about the letter in my bag.

The heavy wooden doors creaked open and a clanging of bracelets heralded Madeleine in another nautical outfit, red scarf tied at a jaunty angle around her neck.

She lit up at the sight of my father. 'I've finally caught you, Bill. You must come in and have a drink with me – I won't take no for an answer.'

'A cool one would certainly do the trick,' Dad said. 'How about my sergeant?'

Madeleine looked at Eugene like he was a species she hadn't encountered. 'There's a tap by the tank stand.'

I waited for Dad to speak up for Eugene, but Madeleine had already pulled him into the hallway. He looked as uncomfortable as he had on the Twister mat.

'I'm actually here to see Don.'

'What a shame he's not around at the moment. Looks like I've got you all to myself.'

'It's important. I need to fill him in, man to man.'

Madeleine sighed. 'He'll turn up eventually. He always does.'

I tried not to stare as Madeleine led us past purple orchids spraying out from a pair of crystal vases. A striking Eastern archway separated the living area from the dining room and both rooms were full of heavy oak furniture. There was a Persian rug on the floor, the first rug I'd ever seen in PNG. Everything in this house was so permanent. I imagined the armies of workers who must have hauled it all into place, like the pyramids of Egypt.

Madeleine finally acknowledged Rosie and me as we shuffled around. She embraced my sister like a long-lost daughter and then looked at me in that familiar, slightly disappointed way. She clasped my hands between her bracelets like a consolation prize. 'Billie, I'm delighted you were able to come down with Rosie. She's a favourite here, you know.' She peered at me. 'You'll have a chance to change later.'

'Billie doesn't go in for dressing up, Mummy.' Vanessa breezed into the room. 'Don't worry, you look fine.' She spoke in a conspiratorial tone, like it was us against her mother.

Madeleine turned her gaze onto her daughter. Vanessa had on a *meri* blouse, but on her it actually looked good, hanging elegantly off her shoulder and barely covering her long thighs.

'Well, *you* certainly need to change, young lady. And what's that around your neck?'

It was a shark's tooth and straight away I knew where it'd come from.

'A Christmas present from a friend, Mother.'

'Well, it's a little native, dear. Take it off before the rest of the guests arrive.'

Madeleine sat on the Chesterfield and patted the seat next to her. 'Make yourself at home, Bill, while the boys get us a cocktail. What do you fancy?'

Dad shook his head. 'I'm on duty. You better give me a squash.'

'It's the weekend, for heaven's sake, Bill.' Madeleine turned to us. 'Why don't you girls go and meet some of the other guests.'

The other two disappeared through a doorway at the far end of the room, but I hovered, not wanting to let my father out of my sight.

Sensing my reluctance, he turned to Madeleine. 'Billie's a bit upset by all the argy-bargy out on the island. I thought I might pop across for another word with the blokes involved and she's worried.'

'I can understand that. The louts who took over the jetty *are* frightening, especially the ringleader. They say he goes to university down south – *there's* the thanks we get for educating these people.'

Dad grinned. 'Funny you should say that, because it's the *old* one Billie's worried about. I think she's a bit sweet on the young fella.'

I felt my cheeks redden.

'How extraordinary.' Madeleine fixed her cool green eyes on me.

I thought of the letter inside my bag and how easily I could have wiped the smirk right off her face. I turned and headed off in search of the other two, before the temptation got too much for me.

Finding them was harder than I expected. The house was a labyrinth of corridors, verandahs and doors that seemed to go nowhere. I found myself in a corridor with a long row of framed sepia photos on the wall. Family groups dressed in tropical white stared stone-faced at the camera. Further along, glass cases filled with artifacts like ivory carvings and shells stood in rows like a real museum. History lay heavy in the air.

A low voice at my side made me jump. 'Missus, you likim onepela drink?'

It was a local girl in a white *meri* blouse and *lap-lap*. I nodded gratefully and she disappeared through a flywire door onto the back verandah.

Through the wire, I glimpsed a conga line of

workers carrying piles of napkins, bundles of cutlery, bowls of flowers, baskets of fruit, even a jukebox hoisted by half a dozen puffing men.

I wandered over to the glass cases and one caught my eye. It was a collection of personal effects, some shrine to a long-dead pioneer: a battered cream hat, a monocle and a pocket watch, even a large monogrammed handkerchief. As I leant forward to take a closer look, a memory of the little man chanting over a piece of white cloth lurched into my mind and I realised what the white cloth had been. Tobias had taken Dad's handkerchief and used it in some kind of magic ritual. I had to warn my father.

The wire door squeaked and the girl held out a crystal tumbler. I gulped down the squash, trying to look appreciative as I passed the glass back and turned on my heel.

Backtracking along the corridors, I heard male voices and caught a glimpse of green billiard table through an open door. I peered in, and all eyes turned to me.

'Don't bother with Billie,' Stuart called out. 'That'd be cradle snatching.'

A chorus of guffaws rang out as a blond boy stepped into the corridor and held out his hand. 'Hi, I'm Angus Rivers. Ignore my friends.'

'Don't worry, I will.'

So, this was the 'spunky' Angus. He had a pleasant enough face, but he didn't have Errol's sizzle.

Rosie sidled up and tapped Angus on the shoulder. 'I'll look after my little sis.'

He shrugged and went back into the billiard room, although it seemed like he'd sought me out for a reason.

Rosie put her hands on her hips. 'Where'd you get to? You'll never meet anyone hiding around the corridors, you know.'

'They're not my type.'

'They're the best you're going to get. By the way, Dad said goodbye.'

'What?'

'He popped in just now, said he couldn't wait any longer.'

My stomach plummeted. 'Why didn't you come and find me?'

'What's the panic?'

I ran back towards the kitchen, banged through the screen door and ran along the verandah to the back steps, which I took two at a time, before streaking across the lawn and down the hill. An overhanging frond slapped my face as I kept running, but as I sprinted towards the launch area, the wake of a speedboat was clearly visible ahead, splitting the strait.

# Chapter 19

## Vanessa's party

I slumped down on one of the copra bags outside the shed. On the far side of the Statesman I caught a glimpse of Errol's Fastback, deep in the shadow of a palm tree; he must have driven back down the night before. The humiliating moment on Desmond's divan came flooding back – the smell of sandalwood, the feel of Errol's skin against mine and the taste of shame.

'Hello, young Billie.' Don's booming voice made me jump. 'What are you doing down here?'

'I wanted to speak to Dad before he went out to the island but he gave me the slip.' I pointed at the line of wake.

Don looked puzzled. 'Why would he go out there on the weekend alone?'

'He'd found something out. But he wasn't alone; he had Sergeant Eugene.'

'And he didn't bother talking to me beforehand?'

'He stayed around for a while but he must have thought he was running out of time.'

'Don't look so worried, girl. We can keep an eye on him. I've got a telescope on my roof.'

Don huffed and puffed up the path in front of me, looking slightly comical in shorts, but clearly still the *masta*, as everyone we passed nodded in deference. He led me up the rear steps into the house and turned into a little passage I hadn't seen before. A narrow staircase led upwards at a steep angle. He struggled up heroically, pausing halfway 'for a breather'.

At the top a tiny room with an open window, hardly bigger than a crow's nest on a ship's mast, faced out to sea. Don peered down the telescope and angled it correctly for me. I focused in on the back of my father's head, then panned out to the plantation worker driving the speedboat and Sergeant Eugene perched alongside.

'It's a great view,' I said.

'Vanessa loves it too. She's always up here.'

I wondered if she signalled Errol from the lookout. Perhaps they had a secret meeting place somewhere on the plantation and he waited for her signal.

The boat jumped out of the frame as it bumped over the waves, and by the time I'd found it again, it was approaching the jetty. My hands were sweating as I struggled to keep the telescope steady and flashes of sea and bush bumped in and out of view.

'I can't see.'

'Let me have a go.' Don fiddled with it. 'There he is.'

I put my eye back on the lens just in time to see Dad disappear into the shade of the palm trees. While I'd had him in my sights, he was safe. Now it was like he'd fallen off the edge of the world.

'Don't worry. Your father knows how to take care of himself.'

As I was making my way back into the house along the rear verandah, I ran into Vanessa and Rosie and the half-dozen boys following in their wake.

Vanessa smiled sweetly. 'You'll come for a quick dip, won't you, Billie?'

Spending time with Vanessa and her band of admirers was the last thing I wanted to do, but I didn't want to make a scene so I grabbed my swimmers from the bag. Vanessa led us down the hill, past the shed to the beach. I watched her closely as she passed the Fastback but there wasn't even a flicker of recognition. Hardly surprising really; she had to be pretty sly to have kept their secret for so long.

'You boys can get changed in the shed,' she announced. 'We'll go behind the trees up there.'

Rosie and I exchanged a confused glance as we followed Vanessa to a clump of palms further up the beach; the reverse arrangement would have made more sense. Even my sister looked uncomfortable when Vanessa dropped her shift and stood out in the open dressed only in a pair of skimpy knickers. My mother would have been horrified. She'd always drummed into us how careful we had to be not to inflame the passions of the local men. I couldn't help noticing Vanessa's skin had an all-over golden glow.

'Stop showing off,' Rosie said.

Vanessa giggled as she wriggled into her swimmers. I huddled behind a narrow trunk, as I guessed Vanessa was parading for an imaginary Errol, rather than Angus and his schoolboy friends peeping around the shed door. Her eyes were fixed on the island, and I wondered if it drove her mad, knowing he was out there and not being able to reach him.

Vanessa dipped her feet in the water and began to splash Rosie, who squealed obligingly, as the cluster of boys headed in their direction. The way Vanessa toyed with males was so irritating that I dived in and swam out to deeper water. To my surprise Angus followed me out.

'Hey, can I have a quiet word with you?' He trod water beside me.

I shrugged.

'You live in Kavieng, don't you? Vanessa disappeared for ages there the other day, when she was supposed to be with me. You wouldn't know what she was up to, would you?'

I was worried he might see me blush but he just kept babbling.

'No, of course you don't. It was a crazy idea ...' He glanced back at the group near the beach. 'Hey, do me a favour, don't tell the others?'

He swam back. I squinted across the water towards the island but the aqua horizon was blank. Images of where my father might be and what he might be doing kept surfacing in my mind but he remained out of focus. It was a relief when we traipsed back up the hill.

The party was, of course, like nothing I'd ever seen before. The sound of the gong caught me unawares, as I was heading down to check whether the speedboat had returned. People appeared from all directions and I was caught up with the guests filing into the lounge room. Through the arch we could see the dining table set with white linen and candles. Outside, coloured lights and bamboo flares awaited the darkness. We stood sipping punch from crystal glasses like we'd done it all our lives.

I checked my reflection in a big gilt-edged mirror and was relieved to see that the envelope I'd hidden in the bodice of my dress wasn't obvious. After a few minutes, Madeleine led in her daughter and the room hushed. Vanessa was dressed in a red plunging halter-neck dress and the shark tooth was still around her neck.

As the houseboys in white *lap-laps* led us to the table, Vanessa's aunt, Sybil, joined us.

She was quite different to her sister-in-law. Sybil dressed like a worker, and tonight she had on a plain blouse and a gym skirt. As she and Madeleine nodded to each other, their mutual dislike was clear.

'I haven't held you up, have I?' she asked, not quite apologising. 'The damnedest thing happened this after-noon. I was getting the mail together when I noticed one of the envelopes had ripped open. When I picked it up, a finger fell out on my desk.'

She paused for dramatic effect.

'How awful for you,' Madeleine said.

'Worse for the owner of the finger, I imagine. We found

the poor bugger in one of the copra bags. The policeman from Conos has only just finished taking our statements.'

'Bill and his sergeant were here just a few hours ago,' Madeleine said. 'What a pity you didn't let us know.'

Sybil shook her head. 'No need for the big guns. Just a simple payback thing; his wantok had been killed by a tractor driven by one of their wantoks. The poor devil was only doing what his family demanded – and sending home the proof.'

The houseboys shuffled in and placed prawn cocktails in front of us. Anything served in a tall glass was the height of glamour to me. As Sybil dragged a plump, pink tail out of the glass, she chuckled. 'I hope I haven't put you all off your dinner.'

After we'd finished our steaks, Vanessa slipped away from the table and I followed, hoping to catch her alone. She went down yet another corridor and stopped in a doorway.

Her father's voice boomed out, 'Princess.'

'Daddy, you're going to miss the food if you don't hurry.'

'I'm sorry. Time gets away from me in here.'

'Aunty Sybil's here. She told a disgusting story about finding a finger in the mail.'

'Trust Syb to spoil your mother's party.'

They chuckled together.

Feeling like an eavesdropper, I coughed and walked towards them.

Vanessa drew me into the small room. 'Come and say hi to my father, Billie. He's hiding out in his den.'

A few stools stood in front of a beige padded bar. The room was small, windowless and stifling.

'What's your poison?' Don's face was red but there was a twinkle in his blue eyes.

'I'll have a Pimm's and lemonade, Daddy, and Billie will have the same.'

Don's tongue poked out of his mouth as he filled two tall glasses with ice and what looked like fizzy red cordial and carefully set them in front of us.

'Well, I'd better say hello to my sister or I'll be in trouble.' He shuffled off.

We sat sipping for a few minutes. My stomach was tight but I had to say something. 'I know where you got your shark tooth.'

'Okay, you've sprung me. It was a Christmas present, which is quite sweet, really.'

Seeing her act so normal was unsettling but I still wanted to shake her. 'I don't get you, Vanessa. You wear his necklace, but you haven't got the guts to invite him to your party?'

'You're so *romantic*, Billie.' She spat it out like an obscenity. 'You think I'm rich, I'm free to do what I want, but there are a lot of things you don't understand. Like, for a start, who owns all this stuff?'

I shrugged.

'My uncle, Roger, that's who. Didn't you notice the initials RW on their lap-laps? Everything we have, we have because Uncle Roger gives it to us. In return, I go to Frensham, look pretty and marry one of those boys out there. Errol isn't part of the deal. I mean, can you really see Errol sitting comfortably in all of this?'

I pulled the envelope out and put it on the bar in front of her.

She looked rattled. 'How did you get this?'

'Desmond gave it to me. Errol accidentally dropped it in his store.'

Turning her back to me, she ripped the envelope open and read the letter in gulps, taking in a few words, holding it to her chest and pulling it up to her face again. I looked away, embarrassed by her emotion. It didn't really matter what the letter said. They were mad for each other and there was no point kidding myself anymore.

Vanessa was already on her way out a wire door leading onto the side verandah. 'I've got to go. Do me a favour, say you haven't seen me.'

As she disappeared into the trees leading down to the jetty, I looked out and saw the red sun hovering above a grey sea.

194

# Chapter 20

## The Statesman returns

When I got back to the table, Madeleine was fussing around next to a multi-tiered birthday cake. 'Where on earth is the birthday girl?' she asked.

'She was with Billie in my bar when I last saw her,' Don said.

Every head at the table seemed to turn in my direction.

'Where is she then, Billie?' Madeleine demanded.

I felt my cheeks burn. 'I've got no idea. I went to the toilet and just assumed she'd be back here by now.'

'How very odd.' Madeleine rubbed her temples with her fingers and closed her eyes.

There was an awkward silence before she clapped her hands together. 'I've got something much more exciting than cake. Follow me.'

She led us out to the verandah where a large chrome jukebox sat in state like a Wurlitzer organ. She pushed a button and Lesley Gore started belting out 'It's my party'.

'Isn't it a beauty,' she shouted above the noise. 'Don had it shipped over from the Cecil Hotel. It's got all the classics, Chuck Berry, Elvis, you name it.'

She grabbed the arms of a couple standing nearby and pushed them towards the music.

Vanessa didn't return and I wondered where she and Errol were hiding. Angus paced around looking lost and I avoided his questions by dancing with a succession of sullen boys. I wasn't sure whether my father would return to the party or head straight home, so I was relieved when a set of headlights wound their way up the hill. Dad was back.

The car jerked to a halt next to the fountain. I rushed to meet my father but it was Sergeant Eugene who jumped out the driver's side. Blood dripped from a gash across his forehead and he was looking back down the hill as though someone was chasing him. 'Oligeta man i-go crazy. Fightim me ...'

I went cold. 'Where's Dad?'

'Mi no savvy.'

'What do you mean, you don't know?'

'I try to find him, miss, but men beat me, throw me long speedboat.'

I turned to the crowd that had gathered around us, desperate for help, but they seemed to recoil.

'Mr Barry,' I screamed. 'Come quickly, the sergeant's hurt. I think something's happened to Dad.'

Rosie appeared from the darkness. 'What did you say about Dad?'

'It's Sergeant Eugene. He says Dad's missing, somewhere on the island.'

The music from the jukebox stopped suddenly and the last sentence hung in the silence. Rosie's bottom lip quivered as she lurched towards me. Her arms tightened around my neck, and I thought of the drowning who drag their rescuers down with them.

Don waddled into the light. 'Let's try to keep our heads. Come inside, Sergeant.' He ushered us into the lounge room and spoke to the men in *lap-laps*. 'Kisim Missus Sybil.'

He held a hand towel out to Eugene. 'Something to stop the bleeding until my sister can bandage your head.'

'Thank you, Masta.' Eugene held it against his temple.

'Now try to answer calmly. When was the last time you saw Masta Bill?'

Eugene's eyes were bloodshot. 'Masta told me guard

boat, he must tok to young fella. He say maybe long time, no worry. When sun go down, me think time to find masta.'

Don looked incredulous. 'So, you just sat with the boat until dark?'

Eugene's face twisted and his shoulders heaved with emotion.

Don shook his head impatiently. 'Go on, man, go on.'

Eugene took a deep breath. 'Me get torch, walk long track to spirit house. But men block track. One man take torch, hit me.'

'Who were these men?' Don asked.

Eugene shook his head. 'Mi no savvy. Emi dark, plenty man around.'

'Where's your firearm, Sergeant?' Don squinted at him.

Eugene grimaced. 'One man took it.'

'There's an awful lot you don't know about what's happened. You don't know who hit you, you don't know who stole your gun, you don't know even where the DC is, for God's sake.'

Eugene leant forward, his eyes flashing. 'Kisim plantation men, let's go long island, findim masta.'

Don crossed his arms. 'Nobody's setting foot on that island until we get reinforcements.'

'Please, Mr Barry. Dad might be lying out there hurt somewhere.'

But Don was already walking towards the door. 'I'll arrange for a driver to take you girls home.'

Rosie and I clung to opposite sides of the back seat as we sped along the black road. I knew I should hold her, comfort her, but I couldn't. Ever since Sergeant Eugene had got out of the car instead of my father, fear had me in its grip. Flashing past the windows the jungle made crazy, distorted shapes and I squeezed my eyes closed against them.

I was plagued by thoughts that it was all my fault. My mantra – *Please God, let him be okay, please God, let him be okay* – echoed in the rhythm of the wheels. It was like being in suspended animation, travelling through the blackness in this metal capsule, and I wished it would go on forever. When we got home there'd be no more pretending, and I dreaded the sight of my mother's face more than anything.

When we'd been driving for what felt like hours, the car rounded a bend and I realised we were on the outskirts of town. The dread moved to my stomach.

'Please stop.' My voice came out as a whisper, as it had in my dream. I tugged on Rosie's arm.

She leant forward and tapped the driver's shoulder.

'Hey. My sister needs to stop. Now!'

I threw the door open and the prawn cocktail slid up my throat and splattered across the undergrowth.

I wiped my mouth and we carried on. After a couple more minutes, the car pulled into our driveway and the headlights picked out Mum standing next to the front door. Had she been there for hours, I wondered, wringing her hands like someone in a Greek tragedy, with her hair flowing down like a crinkly brown shower curtain?

The three of us clung together, with the driver standing back awkwardly.

'Oh, girls …' Mum paused to collect herself. 'Let's go inside and sit down.'

The house looked strange. A couple of small lamps threw an eerie green wash over everything. Mum sank into the couch and Rosie and I sat on either side of her.

Mum choked on her words. 'Girls … we must prepare ourselves for the worst. Nathan said as much. He was on his way down with as many police as he could muster. A contingent is coming across from Rabaul at first light and the Police Commissioner's flying in from Moresby.'

Morning brought activity. Knocking began at our door as soon as it was light and a procession of women appeared, making cups of tea and cooking breakfasts that none of us could stomach. It was as though our kitchen had become the headquarters of an emergency operation.

Martha came too, waiting shyly to be invited in. I was immediately reminded of the charmed circle she'd shared with my father only a few nights ago. I took her hand and led her into the kitchen, and she was soon bustling with the rest of them.

Max appeared on our back verandah looking and smelling as if he'd spent the night drinking rum.

'Why didn't he take my trawler? With a cargo of polis? Instead of going down like the Lone Ranger with Tonto.' He paced up and down, muttering.

When Max left, Mum disappeared in the direction of her bedroom. She'd wandered aimlessly through the morning, leaving a trail of barely touched teacups in her wake, so I went in to see if she needed help. She was sitting on the edge of the bed holding the wedding photo in the silver frame that normally sat on the bedside table. The authority that had intimidated me my whole life had evaporated overnight.

I gently coaxed her into the bathroom and ran the shower. I was walking back down the passage when I heard her calling my name in a panicky voice. She stood at the door, dripping onto the passage floor and trying to cover herself with a towel.

'What is it, Mum?'

'Susan, where's Susan?'

'She's down at the nuns' clinic, remember? A car's been sent, she'll be here soon. Pop back in the shower and I'll get your house coat.'

Susan soon appeared at the front door. Her hair was pushed back from her face with bobby pins, like she hadn't had time to fix it.

'Thank God you're here.' I lowered my voice, 'Mum is falling apart. I've never seen her like this.'

'What do you expect me to do about it?'

I was stunned into silence.

'Mum acts tough, but Dad's her rock. If he's gone, she'll have nothing. I can't fix that.'

# Chapter 21

## Certainty

Time moved on a different trajectory that day. The minutes ticked as slowly as the sweat dripping down our legs as we squirmed on the couch or paced the lounge room waiting for news. But when certainty arrived, the minutes were shunted forward with such force that everything shattered.

A policeman stood at the door, his chest fluttering with coloured ribbons. It was strange to see the uniform I associated so strongly with Eugene being worn by a man with knobbly pink knees.

'Commissioner ...'

'The name's Blake, Mrs Cleary. We met at the last annual conference in Moresby.'

'Yes, yes, I remember.'

'Won't you come inside, sir?' Susan took Mum's arm and we followed her and the Commissioner into the lounge.

'We should sit down.' Susan ushered the policeman over to my father's armchair and the rest of us squashed onto the couch. We all turned to him. He held his cap in his hands and I couldn't take my eyes off it as he twisted it backwards and forwards.

'There's no gentle way to say this. I regret to tell you that a body has been found, and we have reason to believe it is that of your husband.'

Rosie began to whimper.

'Oh,' my mother whispered; a tiny sound a child might make. She closed her eyes and I thought for a moment that she was going to faint. 'How?'

'I'm not at liberty to discuss the details before the autopsy, but … it appears he was stabbed.'

We all gasped.

'How did it take so long to find him?' Susan said. 'Maybe if they'd been quicker …'

'An attempt had been made to conceal the … remains by dragging them into the bush and covering them with a large branch.'

I closed my eyes and saw blood seeping into dirt.

My mother made a choking noise.

'*He's* our father and her husband – not remains,' Susan snapped.

'Nonetheless …' The Commissioner handed my mother a freshly ironed handkerchief. 'His deputy, Nathan Sigeri, has made the formal identification, but if you wish to view … your husband, they'll be bringing him back on the trawler about six o'clock and he'll be kept at the hospital, pending an autopsy.'

'Did Nathan arrest anyone?' I blurted.

Everyone turned to me.

'I beg your pardon. Miss Cleary, I presume.'

'My name's Billie. I was afraid something would happen to him, ask my mother.'

My mother sighed and shook her head. 'Not now, Billie.'

The Commissioner drew himself up. 'Your mother's right, young lady. We need to talk about the necessary arrangements. Mrs Cleary, have you given any thought to where you would like …'

Susan bristled. 'You're unreal – you know that? You've just told us our father's dead, and you're already asking—'

'Bill wants to stay here,' my mother interrupted.

We all looked at her with surprise. She had battled with this country for my father's heart; we weren't expecting her to give up his body so easily.

'We spoke about it recently. He wants to be cremated. I wasn't expecting that. He was brought up Roman Catholic, you see … but he said if anything happened to him, he wanted to stay in this country. He even told me where. It was his favourite place …'

My sisters and I reached for her hands. We looked at each other and together we saw the channel between the two islands and the tide that would draw the ashes out into the ocean.

My mother stood abruptly, wrenching her hands out of our grasp. 'Oh Lord. What am I going to tell his parents?'

'They'll be officially notified because he died on duty. It's protocol.' The Commissioner stood and turned with a neat click of his polished shoes. 'I'll leave you to grieve privately.'

It didn't seem right that one of the office johnnies that my father so despised should be in charge of laying him to rest. I wanted to slap the man for trying to smooth over our pain and questions so neatly. He didn't even seem to care who had killed him.

One by one, the crew in the kitchen took their leave, snuffling and embracing my mother and each other before walking quickly away.

Martha was the last to leave and she lingered in a way that showed she didn't really want to go. I could hardly believe she was the same woman who had stood in the shadows a few nights before. She and Mum shuffled together in the doorway for a long time.

'Don't worry, you'll be fine,' Mum said.

It seemed an odd comment until I realised she was handing the mantle of DC's wife to Martha. The unexpected kindness seemed to catch Martha off guard and she wept as she made her way down the path.

'Mum, you should take something to help you sleep. I have some tablets from the clinic,' Susan said.

'Why would I want to sleep in the middle of the afternoon? I need to be there when he gets back.'

Mum agreed to lie down but only if we promised to call her the minute the trawler came into view.

Once she was settled, I sat on the bunker looking out at the harbour with the strange feeling that all the previous times I'd sat there had been a rehearsal for this day. My mind was churning. I squeezed my eyes closed, trying to picture my father's face, but he wouldn't come. I felt like I'd failed him already, lost him in a day. Then I heard his voice again, his big booming voice telling me not to be so damn stupid, and I smiled to myself.

My eyes traced the path of a small canoe as it made its way back into harbour. It began to rock as it approached a pier down the far end of the town, and I followed the line of the wake back and saw the trawler already well into the harbour.

Damn. I'd missed that moment when the trawler rounded the corner of the island, and now I'd have to rush to wake my mother. The tears I'd been expecting earlier took me by surprise then, running down my cheeks as I ran towards the house.

'Mum, wake up.' I ran headlong into her bedroom. She rolled over, her hair messy across her eyes like a young girl. It would have been kinder to leave her there in that limbo land, but behind me I felt the trawler ploughing across the harbour, so I shook her shoulder. The pain crossed her face as she remembered that my father was dead. Her lip quivered and I dropped down next to her so I could hold her hand. 'Don't worry, Mum, I'll be with you, but the boat's coming in. We should hurry so we can be down at the wharf before it docks.'

I led her out the front, where Julius was leaning on the car. Nathan must have sent him to fetch Mum.

'Julius,' I said, 'we need to be down at the wharf in time to meet the trawler – can you get us there quicktaim?'

He gave me a grim smile.

As the car began to move off, I remembered my sisters and wound down the window.

'Rosie … Susan … Rosie.' My voice had a high, hysterical note to it. I couldn't understand why they weren't here. Didn't they know we had to be there to meet Dad?

Tahl came running out the front door and I shouted to him, 'Tell the girls we'll meet them at the haus sik.' My stomach was tight with panic but there was a calm edge to my thinking that surprised me. I felt as though Dad was depending on me and I had to think clearly for him.

Just then the girls ran past Tahl in the doorway; Rosie, curls bouncing and breathless, Susan carrying Mum's handbag.

Susan opened the back door of the car and slid in on the other side of Mum.

Rosie jumped into the front seat and immediately turned to snap at me. 'You were going to drive off and leave us, weren't you? Honestly, since … this has happened, it's like you and Mum are the only ones grieving.'

My cheeks flushed because I knew she was right. I had mentally shut the other two out, as though they didn't exist.

'We went to get her bag.' Susan unclasped it. 'She'd want to look her best, Billie.'

She passed Mum her lipstick and gold compact and began to twist her hair into a bun. Mum's hand shook and she smudged the lipstick, but after Susan carefully slid a pair of tortoiseshell sunglasses onto her nose, the transformation was amazing. She was almost back to the mother I knew. Just the greyness of her skin against the familiar coral lipstick gave her away.

My window was open; I leant my face into the breeze and closed my eyes tight. I couldn't look at the road, the trees, the sea, at any of the things that had been so dear to me before yesterday. They were part of a world that had been shattered. I wanted to stay gently bouncing against my mother's body, without thought or fact.

For as long as I could remember, my mother had tried to change me, as though my very existence was a disappointment to her. Now it was my job to take care of her. My sisters were right. I should have thought of the bag. From that point on, it was up to me to think like she would and do everything I could to spare her pain.

The car jolted and I felt the rhythmic bumps as it drove across the planks of the wharf. Julius was driving right up to the gangway. I guessed that he was trying to shield my mother from as much exposure as he could, and I silently blessed him for that.

The throb of the trawler motor dropped an octave as it idled into position for the final approach. I steeled myself and slowly opened my eyes.

In the few minutes since I'd closed them, the setting sun had thrown a mauve blanket over the world. There was a softness to the air that brought a lump to my throat. The place was putting on one last beautiful show for my father.

Then I saw Sergeant Eugene. The trawler was only twenty feet or so out, coming in nose first, and he stood at the very front. He didn't react as the boat's crew darted around him, ready to fling the heavy rope across to the waiting men on the wharf. His head was bowed, his shoulders hunched, his hands rested on top of a rifle. He stood lonely as a statue.

# Chapter 22

## Haus sik

An insistent tapping broke into my thoughts. Commissioner Blake was knocking on Susan's window.

'They're waiting for us, Mum,' Susan said. When my mother didn't move she tried again. 'Mum, the *Comm-issioner's* waiting for you.'

My mother continued to sit motionless.

I squeezed her hand. '*Dad's* waiting for us, Mum. He's on the boat and we've come to say goodbye to him, do you remember?'

Her thighs made a squelching sound on the vinyl as I eased her across the seat and out the door. She swayed a little as she got to her feet and my sisters put an arm under her elbows. Commissioner Blake motioned us to the edge of the gangway.

Nathan was already standing there. His glance slid across us and came to rest more comfortably on the Commissioner. The men saluted each other and Nathan spoke to my mother without looking at her. 'I'm so sorry, Mrs Cleary. Your husband was … the best. I can't believe this has happened to him, of all men.'

Sergeant Eugene stood at the top of the gangway. He turned towards us and saluted slowly. Then he took one step back and turned sideways.

Behind him a group of policemen clustered around what looked like an awkwardly folded tent canvas lying on the foredeck. They fell into two rows and, on a signal from Eugene, they lifted the canvas to their shoulders and began to shuffle past, a guard of honour.

I tried not to look as the procession passed but my eyes were drawn to the neatness of the large stitches that held the bundle together. Max, the old sailor, must have done it. Perhaps he'd had a few last words to Dad as he yanked the hook through the canvas. He was probably in his cabin, having a rum in honour of his friend. How was it possible that Max, who always looked like he was on his last legs, would have more rums and my Dad wouldn't?

After they shuffled past with downcast eyes, the men moved towards a Land Cruiser parked off to the side. Two men opened the back to reveal a rectangular box of splintery planks, the kind fruit boxes are made from. Except that this box was a coffin. While we had been pacing the morning away, the station carpenter had been quietly building a resting place for my father.

The box was set down on the wharf and the men gently lowered the shroud into it. There was an undignified tussle to close the lid, as though the carpenter had forgotten how tall Dad was. One of the policemen pushed his boot heel down onto the lid until a shout from Eugene stopped him. As they raised the box onto the Land Cruiser, the lid seemed perched loosely on top. In one movement, Eugene leapt onto the tray and held the lid secure as the Land Cruiser pulled away.

'If you would be so kind as to follow us to the hospital, Mrs Cleary, I'll show you where you can wait,' the Commissioner said. 'It will take a little while to prepare … for viewing.'

My mother nodded a weak smile to him. Now that things were on a formal footing, Mum seemed back in familiar territory, and it was *her* leading *us* back to the car.

When we were settled, she turned to us. 'Girls, why

don't we get Julius to take you home? I'll be fine.'

When we were back at the house and my sisters were getting out of the car, I made my case. 'Please let me come with you, Mum?'

Mum nodded, too exhausted to put up much protest. I watched my sisters disappear into the house, looking as they had the first day we'd arrived in Kavieng; Susan, so grown up, leading the reluctant Rosie. Rosie's curls had wobbled as she'd turned back to me, the little sister who always tagged along behind, but Susan had pulled her forward. That was how I was used to seeing my sisters – from behind.

The hospital straddled the headland at the far end of town. By the time our car drew up in front of it, the sun had sunk below the horizon and a dull stillness had flattened the sky and the water below.

The Commissioner beckoned us towards a side entrance and ushered us into a room off the corridor.

'Please wait here, ladies. We still need a little time ...'

I tried not to think about what that might mean as the door creaked closed behind him. Mum slid down onto a metal bench under the louvred windows. Her legs splayed out at an awkward angle, like a Barbie doll abandoned in the middle of a game.

'Mum, are you up to this?'

'It was a beautiful day, the day we were married. Just magic. Unusual for April, everyone said so. I took it as a sign, and I was right. Your father has never let me down.' She fought for a breath. 'And I can't let him down …'

'I'll be there too.'

'Oh no you won't. I won't let you remember your father like this. That's the least I can do …' She ran her hand down my face. 'I know I've been hard on you, Billie …'

The door swung open. Behind it stood a man in a white cap and gown, white mask hanging from his neck. It took me a second to recognise the doctor.

My mother and I jumped up.

Mister Sid grasped her hand. 'I'm so sorry, Jocelyn.'

It was strange hearing my mother called by her first name; I'd almost forgotten she had one. My father always called her darl and everyone else called her Mrs Cleary.

'Can I get you something before you go in?' It sounded like he was offering her a cocktail at a party until he nodded towards a glass-fronted cabinet full of pill bottles.

My mother shook her head. 'I have to remember this. It's all I'll have left.'

'If it's any consolation, he looks at peace. The damage was very localised.'

The contrast between the doctor's silky English accent

and the horror behind his words made me shiver. I didn't want to wait alone in the cold fluorescent glare, imagining what Mum was seeing in the room along the corridor. I headed out the door into the dark and immediately felt the peace of invisibility around me.

I moved further into the darkness towards the unrelentingly black cove beyond. The only light came from what looked like a chalky white rock off to the left. As I walked closer, its edges sharpened into a rectangle and I saw it was a tombstone, one of a cluster of graves that had slid sideways into the sandy soil. I was leaning forward trying to read the words carved into it when a cough from behind made me jump.

'Yu orright, Miss?'

It was Julius. He held a large metal torch out to me. 'Yu lukim hul bilong plainim man?'

A hole to plant a man in – what else would you call a grave?

The torchlight picked out the words. *Johannes Myer. 1887-1912.*

Some twenty-five-year-old German colonist had died a long way from home. I hoped he hadn't been stabbed on a lonely bush track.

The glow of a campfire across the water caught my eye.

It was comforting to think of people gathered around it, cooking or warming themselves. So much better for Dad to be swirling out there on that warm evening tide than stuck in a hole like poor Johannes.

I remembered Mum with a thud of guilt. As I approached the hospital, the door burst open and Mum loomed in front of me.

'Billie.' She pulled me sideways into the shadows. 'He was too perfect. There's something they're not telling me.' She ran her finger down my t-shirt. 'The front of his shirt sat down flat just the way I ironed it yesterday morning.'

'Mum.' Something in her voice was scaring me. I managed to get her back inside the brightly lit entrance.

Her eyes widened with shock. 'When Sid turned around, I rolled Bill over. There was this little black hole in his back. I can't believe that was what killed him – it looked so tiny.'

'Mum, come and sit down inside for a second.'

'How could anyone do that to him?' Her lip quivered as the doctor came up beside her and quietly injected something into her arm.

# Chapter 23

## Bad dream again

Mister Sid had insisted on driving us home from the hospital and settling my mother. Now he sat across the kitchen table from me, explaining in his calm British voice how my mother's reaction was to be expected.

He rummaged in his bag as he spoke and just for a moment I felt panic. Perhaps my mother was right, perhaps there was a conspiracy around my father's death?

But then I remembered that time Mister Sid was drinking squash at the Golf Club and Dad turned on a man who'd muttered about 'poofter drinks' and said, 'The doc's fair dinkum.'

Mister Sid held a handkerchief out to me, the same kind that Dad had lost on the island. As I dropped my face into my hands, I heard Mister's Sid's light steps retreat.

Somehow, I was back there again, trapped in the spirit house behind the masks, beating my hands on the wood. The stink of pig fat clogged my nostrils, a sickening mixture of lanolin and smelly feet. My hands hurt and my palms were bleeding.

Then I was looking down at the top of my own head and I felt like I was both the butterfly flapping against the glass *and* the collector peering down at it.

I could hear my father's voice, deep and powerful yet muffled through the wood. As his voice receded, I recognised the panic of knowing he was walking into danger and not away from it. I called out but my voice vibrated silently through my throat.

Then I was somehow free of the cage and running to catch my father. I struggled for balance as I tripped down the wooden ladder. My father was just in front of me and I reached out to touch his back. His shirt looked as crisp and flat as a sheet of paper. But as my hand was about to reach him, a tiny spot of blackness appeared in the middle of his back. As I watched, it spread like a blot of ink spilled onto parchment until the blackness covered everything.

I woke in my bed, a vague recollection of Susan having

helped me there sometime during the night. My head was heavy with déjà vu, like the dream was my reality and the days between had been unreal. In the soft dawn light, a copper-coloured gecko climbed slowly along the ridge in the middle of my ceiling. I envied him as he crawled along, no care in the world except getting to the other side.

Everything that morning was tinged with fear. The scream of the flying foxes returning to their homes in the trees, the hibiscus leaves quivering outside my window, even the flicker of the gecko's tail made me breathe faster. Every movement brought back the little man scratching in the dirt in a way not quite human.

When I pushed open the kitchen door, Susan was sitting over a teacup at the kitchen table, as my father had just a few nights earlier.

'I'm off,' I said.

'Where are you going?'

'To see Nathan. We need to find out who did it.'

'Oh, Billie, you've read too many Nancy Drew books. Schoolgirls don't go around solving murders.' Her voice softened, 'Hey, why don't I come with you? I'm more tactful than you and Rosie can keep an eye on Mum.'

Walking down to the offices in the sunshine was the first normal thing I'd done since life changed forever. Everything from now on was going to remind me of Dad. The morning of that first patrol a few weeks ago, when we walked down this path together, it all came flooding back.

Standing in front of the door marked 'District Commissioner' was almost too much. 'Dad's work' had always been a special place, almost sacred. Something about the bookshelves of leather-bound reports and the framed maps on the walls made little girls speak in hushed voices.

I remembered as a five year old sitting on Dad's knee swinging my legs. Some men came into his office dressed for a 'sing-sing' in red and yellow paint and feathers. I must have looked scared because the men all laughed together, Dad as well, but then he put his arm around me. I knew he'd keep me safe, but somewhere along the way he'd forgotten to keep himself safe.

Nathan looked stunned and a little nervous as he ushered us into the office. He'd clearly been too busy to remove the traces of Dad that lingered around the office like aftershave. As we sat down, I was shocked to see the familiar green photo frames still on the desk; fortunately, from where we were sitting, we couldn't see our own faces grinning back at us from a happier time.

Nathan cleared his throat. 'Girls, I'm so sorry …'

'We've come to talk about who did this,' I said.

'We've arrested someone, but I can't talk to you about it.'

'Please tell us.'

'I don't want to upset you …'

'Is it Tobias?'

'It's someone who threatened your father on several occasions. In front of many witnesses.'

My stomach dropped. 'Not Errol?'

Nathan looked uncomfortable.

I struggled to stay calm. 'But Errol tried to *warn* Dad he was in danger. You know that – you were right here in this office when I passed it on.'

'We both know what your father thought of that boy, don't we?'

'Eugene might be able to set you straight.'

'Eugene?' He flicked through some notes on the desk as though he couldn't place the name.

'Sergeant Eugene. He was Dad's right-hand man.'

'He wasn't there when your father needed him, though?'

'That's not fair.'

Nathan looked at his watch and shuffled in his seat.

'At least bring Tobias in and ask him when he last saw Dad.'

'The chief is helping us, as he always does.' Nathan gave me a strange look. 'It'd be better if you stayed out of this. Tongues are wagging out on the island, about yous and this humbug Errol. I'd hate your mother to hear what they're saying.'

Suddenly Susan was lifting me out of the chair. 'Thank you for your time. We'd better get home and check on my mother.'

Outside I turned to Susan. 'What did you do that for? He's making a mistake.'

'If Errol's innocent, they'll figure it out.'

'But he talks tough, like all those boys trying to big-note themselves.' I squeezed her hand. 'Come on, the police station's just a little bit further, let's go see Eugene.'

'I don't s'pose it can hurt.'

As we walked in, the young constable behind the desk looked over his shoulder, as though searching for someone to help him deal with the two strange creatures that had come into his police station. There was only silence back there and a dank smell underneath the fresh tang of burnt sweet potato.

'Mi lookim Sergeant Eugene,' I said.

He looked confused. I tried again.

'Sergeant Eugene. Man bilong DC?'

This time he understood. 'Ah, Ugen. Emi go long haus.'

The door behind us creaked and Commissioner Blake

slid into the room, smiling a little too broadly. 'Ladies. What brings you here?'

'We came to talk to Sergeant Eugene,' I said. 'Just to ask him a few more questions.'

'You've missed him, what a shame. He was so upset, I insisted he take some leave.'

I looked up from the overdone grin to the cold eyes and was sure of one thing; this man didn't care about finding my father's killer.

# Chapter 24

## The prisoner

'Dad took me to the compound where Eugene lives once. It's up there in the bush behind the offices. We could go there right now and see him.'

Susan hesitated. 'I think it's time one of us checked on Mum. Do you think you could manage by yourself?'

I waved her off but I started regretting it as soon as I was alone. Little things flickered just out of the corner of my eye; geckos or maybe rats scurrying through the undergrowth, birds ferreting in the dirt, ants hurrying along logs in single file. Everything was moving around me.

A bird flew up from the undergrowth and the flutter of wings startled me into action. As I ran through the bush, I came upon a set of heavy iron gates. The gates squeaked as I eased them open and stepped onto the crisp white gravel inside.

I may have once been to the compound but there was nothing familiar about the grid of tiny fibro houses sitting neatly behind the gates, each exactly like its neighbour. I was just wondering how I would ever find Eugene when I caught a glimpse of him sweeping the dirt in front of a dwelling not far from me.

He was wearing a navy *lap-lap* secured by his police belt, and as he worked, his chest shone with sweat. He looked more like a prisoner than a policeman.

I was shy with this bare-chested Eugene, but thoughts of my father pushed me forward.

He dropped the broom. 'Miss Billie. What are you doing here?'

'I need to know what happened out there on the island. You're the only one I really trust.'

'Stop, Miss Billie.' He put his face in his hands.

'Nathan said they've arrested Errol. You know he didn't kill my father ...'

Eugene shook his head. 'Mi bush kanaka tasol.'

'What do you mean by that? You're not a bush man; you're a *policeman* and my father respected your opinion. You didn't think Errol was dangerous, I know you didn't.'

'Masta Bill is dead. A Keriva man kill masta. Who cares which one?'

'I care. And you care, you must.'

He glanced towards a young woman standing in the doorway of his house. Her features were strong and handsome like Eugene, and as she turned to study me, the sides of her chestnut-brown face were dappled by a faint black tattoo.

She rocked faster and faster on the balls of her feet but a squawk coming from the string *bilum* slung behind her head grew into a howl. She set it down on the ground and a small child emerged from the tangled cloth within, standing and rubbing its eyes. I tried a reassuring smile, but the woman picked the child up roughly and disappeared back inside. Her anger hit me like a slap. Eugene's eyes were on the ground.

'Is your wife cross with me?'

'Emi fraid tasol.'

'Afraid of what?'

'Emi fraid bigpela masta sackim mi.'

'Why would you be sacked?'

'Job bilong mi lukatim masta. Mi no lukatim masta.'

Eugene's job had been to protect my father, and he hadn't. Made sense his wife was angry that he might have to pay for my father's mistake.

'They're having the funeral tomorrow. Don't let the Commissioner frighten you off – my father would have wanted you there.'

He was still looking at the ground.

'*I* want you there.'

There was a long silence.

As I stumbled along the path back to the coast road, my tears finally fell. Before, I'd felt Eugene would have done anything for us; now I wasn't so sure. And Eugene's wife made me feel it was *me* who had abandoned *him*. Maybe he believed that too. The thought sat like a stone in my stomach.

I don't think I would have noticed Max's trawler if it hadn't let out a short burst on its whistle as it manoeuvred into the wharf.

I watched the Statesman deposit Nathan and the Commissioner at the end of the wharf. Policemen pulled what looked like a sack up from the hold. As they yanked it towards the gangway, I saw it was a man, doubled over and trailing one leg behind him. His arms were bent up behind his back.

One of the policemen kicked the man's feet out from under him and he sprawled face first across the planks of the wharf. The policemen's laughter cracked like a whip across the water. The midday sun reflected off something around the man's neck and I realised with a jolt that it was Errol's shark tooth.

I began to run. I had no plan, except to stop them hurting him. By the time I got to the wharf my heartbeat was thumping in my ears and I had to lean forward for a moment to catch my breath.

The policemen were holding Errol upright. He was barely recognisable. His face was puffed up and the fresh gash on his forehead from the sprawl across the wharf leaked a trail of bright-red blood into one of his swollen eyes. A bruised top lip lifted his mouth into a twisted grin. He was hunched as though his strong body had caved in on itself.

'What have you done?' I shouted.

'This is no place for you,' Nathan said.

'But seeing as you *are* here, you might be pleased to know we have your father's killer,' the Commissioner said.

'*He* didn't kill Dad.'

'We found evidence. *And* he resisted arrest – that's how he came by his unfortunate injuries.'

'I don't believe it. What evidence?'

The Commissioner looked at Nathan. 'The girl's old enough to know the truth.' He turned back to me. 'The boy's own knife was found at the crime scene. It's quite distinctive.'

I remembered the shark tooth insignia glinting on the blade and felt sick.

'I'll get Mister Sid to check on the prisoner,' Nathan said.

I moved closer to Errol so I could wipe the blood off his face with my hanky. 'Why was your knife there?' I whispered.

'Tobias set me up.'

'And why did you run?'

He hesitated for a second, shifting his weight between his feet and I thought perhaps he was going to faint. 'I never meant any of this to happen …'

I felt a hand on my shoulder and Nathan moved between us. 'We need to take the prisoner to the cells. If you'd be so kind …'

They yanked him away from me towards the waiting police wagon. My hand was damp where he'd reached out. I opened it and saw the smear of blood. As they pushed him inside, he turned. 'Let Cedric know. He'll get me out.'

The wagon and the Statesman rolled off the wharf and disappeared up the road, leaving me reeling.

Why had Errol said he *never meant any of this to happen*? Why hadn't he just said he didn't do it, or he didn't know anything about it, or a dozen similar statements of innocence?

I couldn't believe he'd killed my father, but his words suggested he was somehow involved. And by implication, so was I.

# Chapter 25

## Limbo

I wasn't sure how to find Cedric but I remembered Desmond was somehow related to the man. He'd surely know how to contact him and then I wouldn't have to break the terrible news to Lucille.

When I pushed open the door of the Wu Emporium, Shirley was leaning on the counter chatting to Desmond. She stopped mid-sentence and her hand shot up to her mouth.

Desmond stepped out from behind the counter and said my name. The gentleness in his voice told me he knew about Dad.

'I'll get tea.' Shirley disappeared into the back room.

'They've arrested Errol.'

'What for?'

'For Dad ...'

'That's crazy.' Desmond shook his head. 'He never would have done that.'

I'd been telling myself that ever since it happened but somehow hearing him say it made me feel much better.

'It's typical.' His cheeks brightened with emotion. 'He makes a good scapegoat ...'

'He asked me to contact Cedric, but I don't know how.'

'I'll take you.'

Cedric Chan's house was in the old German part of town, past the hospital. The driveway was so overgrown, it felt like we were driving into the jungle. Desmond parked in front of what looked like a concrete bunker obscured by vines. Its stone walls were weathered a dull grey, but when he pushed open the door I saw a sparkling new chandelier hanging slightly askew in the entrance hall. Several green-toned portraits of Asian women on black velvet leant against the walls. Cases of beer and soft drinks were stacked beside them. The place looked more like a warehouse than a home.

'Uncle Cedric?' he called.

A young local girl peered out from a room at the end of the hallway, pulling together the sides of her white towelling dressing gown.

'What is it, young Desmond?' The deep toad-like voice came from behind her shoulder.

Cedric was wearing a matching dressing gown and his hair was slicked back along his scalp. When he saw me, he looked embarrassed.

'I was sorry to hear about your father,' he said in his smoothest politician voice.

'Errol's been arrested and beaten by the police,' I replied.

'What?'

'They found his knife … at the scene. He says Tobias framed him.'

'They're going to be sorry for this.' Cedric turned and headed towards the room the girl had peered out from.

'Don't mention the girl to Errol,' Desmond whispered, as we left. 'He hates Cedric enough as it is.'

'And yet he's turned to him for help?'

'Beggars can't be choosers, I guess.'

'Are you really related to Cedric?'

'My father's a second cousin. None of the family can stand him. He loves to remind them that he's the most successful one. And he's never had the guts to acknowledge Errol. Until now, when he thinks Errol can be someone. You can be sure he won't let anything get in the way of that.'

I thought about these words as Desmond drove me

home. Maybe Cedric had a motive for killing my father. He'd threatened him at our house, although it hadn't seemed serious at the time. But if Cedric was involved, was Errol also implicated?

Desmond pulled up just out of sight of our house. I sat for a moment before I turned to him. 'Promise you'll come and get me if you hear anything.'

He nodded and squeezed my hand. He was the one steady thing amid all the confusion. It was getting harder and harder to say goodbye.

My stomach tightened as I pushed open our front door. The house had been so quiet since Dad had died. It was as though without him the soundtrack of our lives had been turned down. Hushed voices, people sliding silently in and out, emotions kept in tight check and no laughter. It made me want to scream.

My sisters were sitting in the living room with their heads together when I walked in.

'You took your time,' Susan said.

I couldn't tell them about Errol right away.

'How's Mum?' I asked instead.

Susan shook her head. 'Mister Sid's in with her. She's acting strange again.'

'She asked about the funeral as soon as she woke up,' Rosie said. 'I said it was going to be official and we wouldn't have much to do with it, but she started making weird lists, like Dad's favourite songs and his old friends from Coogee.'

Mister Sid emerged from the bedroom a few minutes later. 'She may become agitated now and again. I suggest you take it in turns to sit with her.'

'When will you get the autopsy results?' I asked.

They all looked at me as though I'd said something disgusting.

'I don't think it's appropriate to discuss that with you girls.'

Susan spoke quietly as she escorted him to the door and I knew she was apologising for me.

When she returned, she turned on me. 'How can you be so cold?'

'Why's it cold to want to know who killed him?'

There was a brisk tap at the door.

'I'll get it,' Rosie said.

She came back with Phyllis, who was clutching a straw basket. She pulled each of us into her bosom, dabbing her eyes after each embrace. 'You poor girls. When Sid told me how badly your mother had taken it, I knew I had to come in.'

'You're very kind.' Susan's eyes glistened.

'Did you hear the news? They've got some young thug in the watch house.'

'We didn't know,' Susan said.

Phyllis looked confused. 'But wasn't young Billie down there when they brought him in?'

Three sets of eyes turned on me.

'I didn't think it was worth bothering you with,' I said. 'Errol didn't do it, so they'll have to let him go soon.'

'Why are you so sure he's innocent?' Rosie asked. 'Is it just because you fancy him?'

'Don't be ridiculous. Dad didn't trust Errol. He would never have turned his back on him.'

'So, the boy's innocent because he's not trustworthy? Hardly a convincing defence,' Susan said.

'Did he say anything to you?' Rosie's piercing blue eyes searched my face.

'Just that he was sorry. And he asked me to get Cedric Chan to help.'

'Sorry?' Susan said. 'That doesn't sound like an innocent man to me.'

'So, did you tell Cedric?' Rosie asked.

'I'm just back from there.'

'You told that slimy toad before you told your flesh

and blood?' Rosie said. 'You may think you're in with that Chinatown mob but they're just using you.'

'Come on now, girls, you need to be kind to each other,' Phyllis said. 'Have you had anything to eat?'

Without waiting for a reply, she bustled through to the kitchen with her straw basket.

'She's right,' Susan said. 'You two need to cool it.'

Rosie and I nodded a grudging kind of truce before I followed Phyllis out to the kitchen. There was no sign of Tahl or Suriwan.

'You can't beat sandwiches in a crisis.' Phyllis began pulling things out of her basket – bread, butter, liverwurst, Kraft cheese. I picked up one of the loaves and fingered the Wu Emporium label wrapped around it.

'I'll manage these,' Phyllis said, 'if you can make a pot of tea.'

Five minutes later we were sitting at the table, trying to wash sandwich slabs down with mugs of milky tea.

# Chapter 26

## Preparations

'Make sure you eat the casserole I've left for dinner,' Phyllis said. 'You'll need all your strength tomorrow.'

'The Commissioner hasn't really told us what's going to happen,' I said.

'Good heavens that man's hopeless.' Phyllis rolled her eyes. 'They're having it on the golf course to cope with the numbers. I'm heading back over there now if you want to come with me?'

At the golf course a team of men was building a shelter from bamboo poles and palm fronds on the first tee. A tractor pulling a mower was making pale-green stripes up and down the grass. A squad of prisoners from the local jail were unloading stacks of plastic chairs from a truck, while a couple of warders watched.

Phyllis led me into the clubhouse, where I saw almost every white woman I knew in the town and a few I didn't. Trestles were being set up and covered in tablecloths and trolleys wheeled between the storeroom and the cold room. Plates, cups and glasses were lined up on trays and covered with tea towels.

The buzz of chatter stopped dead as I walked in.

'The poor kids haven't been told what's happening tomorrow,' Phyllis announced. 'I thought Blake owed them that much.'

'He's on the green,' one of the women said.

As I left, the tinkle of glasses started again.

Blake was inspecting the shelter, shaking the bamboo poles with his hand. He blanched when he saw me.

'I was just on my way over to fill you in.'

'When's it going to start?'

'We thought nine. To avoid the heat of the day.'

'And will you want us to say anything?'

He shook his head. 'There is one thing …' For a second he looked like a nervous schoolboy. 'This town has no facilities for cremation. We will have to fly the remains to Rabaul and return the ashes to you the following day.'

I felt the sun beating down on the back of my neck. The Commissioner placed a steadying hand on my arm. 'At the government's expense, of course. Mr Ross has authorised the use of a Caribou.'

The thought of a single urn of ashes rattling around inside such a huge plane was strangely comical. Get a grip, I told myself.

I thought I had imagined the faint sound of laughter as I crunched up the gravel path to our front door. But as I stepped inside I heard it again. The distant giggle got louder as I followed it through the house to the back verandah. Susan and Rosie were sitting around the old rattan table, an open bottle of Negrita and two glasses between them.

'Grab a glass, little sister,' Rosie said. 'Let's bury the hatchet with Dad's favourite tipple.'

'To Dad.' We clinked our glasses. I gasped as the liquor burnt the back of my throat.

'Take it slowly, Billie,' Susan said.

I told them about the cremation. 'I know it's wrong, but the whole thing makes me want to laugh,' I confessed, and then we were all laughing.

'What are we going to tell Mum?' I asked, when the laughter had died down. We looked guiltily at each other.

A thump came from the direction of the bedrooms and I jumped up. 'I'll go.'

Mum was sitting on the edge of the bed when I opened the door. She beamed at me. 'I had a lovely dream. Daddy was playing that game with you girls – the one where he spins you around by the hands – and you were all laughing. It was lovely because I wasn't afraid.' She reached her hand out to me. 'I've been so afraid since it happened.'

'Me too. I was nearly jumping out of my skin this morning.'

'He's left us and he's not coming back. That's what really terrifies me.' Mum picked up the silver-framed wedding photo from the sheets in which it had become entangled and held it out to me. 'Just look at him.'

I'd seen the photo so many times I could picture it with my eyes closed. A young sepia-coloured couple stood with their heads together, cheeks shining and teeth flashing in white sunlight. The woman wore a veil that softened her features, and the man stood strong and upright in his dinner jacket. I stared at my father's face and suddenly he looked like someone I'd never seen before.

'He was very handsome, wasn't he, but I married him for his loyalty. He liked to flirt, but it was just a bit of harmless fun. I knew he'd never leave me.'

A long silence sat uneasily between us. There was so much I wanted to say to her, so many hurts I wanted to take back between us, but it was too hard. She was standing on the edge of a precipice and if I said the wrong thing she might step off.

There was no way I could broach the subject of cremation with her. All I could do was rub her hand over and over again until it felt like sandpaper under my fingers.

'Phyllis brought over some food,' I said. 'Wasn't that nice?'

And then, in case she felt slighted, I added, 'God knows what it'll be. Remember how Dad used to tease her about her weird concoctions?'

Mum smiled weakly.

Susan was standing at the door, holding a cup. 'Here's a tea for you, Mum. You really should try to eat something.'

'A cuppa'll do fine.'

'Then you should rest,' I said. 'The funeral's going to be at nine tomorrow morning, and you're going to need your strength for that.'

A look of panic flashed across her face.

'Don't worry. They're going to do everything – the ceremony, the speeches, everything. We just have to be there.'

Susan picked up the medicine bag she'd left in the

corner. As I retreated, I saw Mum holding her hand out for the tablets like a dutiful child.

When I got back to the verandah, Rosie had already cleared away the glasses. I could hear her moving around in the kitchen but I didn't join her. The mood was broken. We were retreating again into our own shells.

After dinner, Susan said she'd take the first shift. Rosie went to bed and I sat on the verandah, looking out into the darkness. I couldn't stop thinking about Errol in some dank cell at the back of that police station. Nathan had given me his word that the police wouldn't hurt him anymore, but out there somewhere was Tobias and he had magic on his side, magic that Errol believed in.

Something startled me and I realised I'd drifted off. It was midnight already, so I tiptoed into Mum's room and shook Susan. Mum was cradling her face in her hand like a small child, her breath rising and falling steadily.

The old wooden chair next to the bed was hard. Sometime during the night, I slid forward, so when Mum's murmurings woke me near dawn, my head was resting on her chenille bedspread. She was sitting upright, clutching the neck of her nightgown.

'Wake up, Billie. I heard a man whispering out there in

the dark. I was sure they were coming for us, but no matter how hard I tried, I couldn't move or cry out.' She looked at me with horror. 'Am I going crazy?'

'No, Mum. Desmond dropped me off earlier, maybe you heard him saying goodbye. You've had so many sleeping tablets, it's probably all blurring together.'

She grabbed my hand and squeezed it so tight I had to stifle a cry. 'No more tablets. I can't remember anything since the hospital. It's hard to even remember how Bill looked. Tomorrow will be my last chance to say goodbye – please don't take that away.'

'Okay. No more tablets.'

I must have dozed off again, because the next thing I heard was the distant sound of a frying pan spluttering. For a second, I thought Dad was doing one of his fry-ups. Then I remembered.

Susan was standing behind me, a bottle of tablets in her hand. I put my arm across in front of her. 'Mum doesn't want any more.'

'I was just going to give her a Valium. How else is she going to get through it?'

'She said today was her last chance to say goodbye and she wanted to do it with a clear head. I think we should respect that.'

Susan shrugged and backed out of the room. Mum was lying on her back with her arms spread out, breathing lightly through her open mouth. She looked so relaxed I thought I could slip out for a few minutes.

Tahl was bent over the frying pan, but when he tried to hand plates around, my sisters shook their heads. I forced down an orange-yolked egg.

Tahl headed towards my mother's door carrying her favourite Royal Doulton cup. He returned with jerky strides, spilling tea across the floor and looking stricken. 'Missus emi go where?'

The bed was empty, sheets thrown aside. We were looking at each other when Mum's voice behind us made us jump.

'I thought I should clean myself up.' She stood in the doorway in her dressing gown, hair dripping onto the towel around her neck. The wet hair and her moist cheeks made her look younger than she had for years.

Susan helped Mum into her underwear while Rosie dried her hair and pinned it into a tight French roll. We picked out a navy linen dress with a bolero jacket and pillbox hat. As Rosie began applying her makeup, Mum screwed up her face like a child, but she remained still.

I sat watching her for a few minutes, waiting in vain

for some kind of direction. I was so used to my mother at the centre of every family event, directing, delegating and overseeing.

Later, as I stood in the middle of my bedroom, I realised I could wear anything I wanted to my father's funeral. On the back of my chair hung the red and white spotted dress I'd tossed aside yesterday morning. That dress had taken me to Vanessa's party, through the nightmare trip back up the road and our nightlong vigil on the couch with my mother; it felt right that I should wear it now.

# Chapter 27

## The funeral

The first sight of the crowd took my breath away. There was barely a patch of green visible and you could hear the murmur of voices and movement from our front door.

The gleaming Statesman was parked in the driveway, a brand-new Australian flag fluttering on its bonnet. Julius was wearing a new cap trimmed with gold braid and what looked like war medals on his spotless white shirt. When we appeared at the top of the stairs, he hurried around and opened the back door with a shaky arm.

Rosie shot a critical glance at my dress. She was wearing a pale-pink creation and Susan was in beige.

My mother drifted down the stairs and gave Julius a little smile, like a queen favouring one of her subjects. Susan and Rosie propelled her forward. Her outfit was her armour, right down to the white gloves that encased her hands and the court shoes that gave her a slow, regal walk. Her eyes were secure behind tortoiseshell sunglasses.

The girls manoeuvred her into the middle of the back seat between them. I slid into the front seat and exchanged a nervous glance with Julius.

People ran alongside us as the car edged out into the road. As some young boys leant in towards the windows and waved, Julius let out a few short bursts on the horn.

In less than a minute the car stopped on the road closest to the official shelter. We braced ourselves as we stepped out, but, like a miracle, the police parted the sea of people as we worked our way towards the shelter.

Familiar faces came into focus. Tahl, his arm around Suriwan; the trawler's head crewman, shiny chest bare above his black-and-white *lap-lap*; the local librarian with bright combs in her hair; rows of white people sitting on orange plastic seats; the bank johnny with the gold chains sitting next to Mona, who was wearing Yoko Ono sunglasses; Phyllis snorting with grief, and behind her, a purple-faced Max grasping his son's arm. Along from them sat a frosty Madeleine and Vanessa, perfectly beautiful without a trace of makeup. I wondered if she knew about Errol's arrest.

A dais big enough for a couple of rows of seats had been built under the shelter facing the crowd. Commissioner Blake led Mum to an empty seat right in the middle of the front row, between him and a thin white man. The only other vacant seats were behind them, next to Nathan and Martha, so we reluctantly took them.

A wail swept through the crowd as a utility decorated with flowers moved slowly in our direction. On its tray sat a coffin draped with an Australian flag.

I had known my father was dead for two days, but I wasn't prepared for that sight.

The utility stopped and a troop of policemen saluted and raised the coffin onto their shoulders. Eugene was not amongst them. They lowered the coffin onto a plinth that stood between the dais and the people, and the thin man stood and began to speak into a microphone.

'It is with great regret that I come here to honour one of the best officers this country has known.' His voice lifted. 'An officer cruelly cut down in the line of duty …'

The crowd gasped and wept on cue as his voice rose and fell. Weeping would have been a relief, but I couldn't do it. This was a show, something for the crowd that had very little to do with my father. The man sounded too much like the ABC newsreader we listened to at lunchtime, and Dad would have chuckled at the thought of a Moresby bureaucrat singing his praises.

Then I saw Desmond. His light caftan top caught my eye, although he was standing on the very edge of the crowd, right next to the road. He looked unreachable.

The Anglican minister was speaking now, using the same drone that he bored us with every Christmas as he tied things up neatly with religion.

'Death is our final resting place …'

Nobody who spoke really knew my father or understood anything about his death. Eugene should have been standing on that podium, or Max, or even Nathan. I wanted someone to talk about what kind of person Dad was, about the laughs they'd had, even to say that his last mistake had been a fatal one. But the truth wouldn't be allowed to tarnish his perfect image.

A group of local primary school children in mismatched uniforms and bare feet stood up from where they were kneeling in front of the platform. Their voices lifted in that unselfconsciously loud way that only small children have as they sang 'Papua New Guinea, your day has begun …' There were a few raised eyebrows at the choice of the cheery new national song, but I guessed that it was the only one they had ready to perform at a day's notice.

Dad would have been touched.

As the singing continued, the policemen marched forward in formation, lifted the coffin and returned it to the ute tray. The white section of the audience, who had been sitting, stood and suddenly there was no division in the crowd. We were one mass of swaying emotion.

The policemen began to march beside the ute, holding their caps to their chests. There was a ruckus in the crowd and the procession stopped.

A single policeman emerged from the crowd and halted the ute with a raised hand. He threw something out in front of him and the sun caught the brightness of the red and contrasting black. It was the new Papua New Guinea flag. The man carefully smoothed it across the head of the coffin, beside the Australian flag.

He saluted the coffin and placed his own cap down on the flags. There was something familiar about the way he saluted. As he disappeared back into the crowd I realised it was Eugene.

Nathan stepped down off the dais and strode towards the confused-looking policemen, clapping his hands loudly together. The procession slowly resumed. I closed my eyes and let the sounds ebb away. Eugene had given me the image of my father's funeral that I wanted to keep.

When I opened my eyes, I searched out my mother amongst the crowds and saw her making a beeline for the clubhouse.

'What's Mum doing?' I asked.

My sisters followed my glance. Something about the way she was striding out was alarming and we began to rush towards her.

Mum was already shouting at Nathan as we approached.

'Where are you taking my Bill?'

Nathan's response seemed to enrage her. 'What do you mean, Rabaul?'

It was my fault she was making her private pain a public spectacle. I had to stop her.

But she'd given up on Nathan and was rushing towards the clubhouse. 'Where's that weasel Blake?' she shouted.

Commissioner Blake was standing in the shade of the clubhouse, surrounded by a knot of people. Everyone else stepped back as my mother approached at speed.

'Mrs Cleary …'

She knocked away his hand. 'How dare you take my Bill away to Rabaul? You know he wanted his ashes to stay here – I *told* you.'

'I explained to young Miss Billie yesterday that we'd have to take the remains to Rabaul to be cremated.

I *assumed* she'd pass that on to you.' Blake raised his eyebrows and I felt the eyes of the crowd. 'I've put a Caribou at their disposal for the operation.'

My mother was looking at me as though I'd done something awful.

'They're bringing him back,' I croaked. 'We can take him out to the twin islands tomorrow.'

'But don't you understand, I want to be *gone* tomorrow. We need to leave this place as soon as we can.'

I'd been cushioned in shock since the moment Eugene had interrupted Vanessa's party. Although I knew my father was dead, I'd somehow expected my life to go on as usual. But of course we'd have to leave. If not tomorrow, then one day very soon. I'd not only lost my father, I'd also lost my home.

I was suddenly aware of an intense burning pulsing through my body. As I saw the navy linen of my mother's dress slide past my face, I realised I was falling. My last thought before I hit the grass was of Desmond, somewhere out in that crowd.

# Chapter 28

## Ashes to ashes

I opened my eyes and looked out the gap in my bedroom louvres to the red and pink hibiscus fluttering like plump butterflies against a dark green jungle. I hadn't realised how much comfort that view gave me until I was about to lose it.

An uncomfortable memory of vomiting on bright-green grass came to me and the vague impression of strong arms pulling me up. Desmond's sweet face floated back into my mind, and I hoped he hadn't witnessed any of my humiliation.

I'd come to in the back of the official car, Mr Sid beside me, taking my pulse.

'You're in shock, Billie. Nothing a lie down in a cool room won't fix. I'm more concerned about your mother.

She's totally fixated on laying your father to rest, so I've insisted that his remains be returned to her as soon as possible. They've promised this afternoon.'

When we got home, he'd given me something to 'help you rest' before Suriwan had led me to my room. I slumped down on my bed and closed my eyes as she placed a cold face washer across my forehead. I'd dozed until a heavy droning sound forced my eyes open. The Caribou was back.

I made my groggy way along the hallway to the back verandah, where I met my sisters on their way out to the back garden. We stood looking up as the ungainly khaki plane wheeled over on its descent into the airstrip.

Mum came steaming down the stairs. 'I heard a big plane. It's got to be him.'

Susan tried to soothe her. 'Let's get you freshened up and by then the Commissioner will be here.'

'I refuse to let that man take over.'

I felt the heat rising up again. 'I don't think I can go.'

Susan turned to me. 'You know you'll regret it if you don't.'

We waited silently on the back verandah until a Land Cruiser pulled into the driveway. The Commissioner stepped out of the passenger seat, clutching a small metal box, which he held out to my mother. 'Mrs Cleary, it is my solemn duty …'

'Thank you, Mr Blake, but we can take it from here.'

'I've placed every official resource at your disposal.'

'My girls and I will do it our way, thank you.'

He turned and climbed back into the Cruiser with a sulky mouth.

Mum lifted an imperious finger and Julius slowly drove forward from where he'd been parked under a tree.

I pushed my face deep into the vinyl padding of the car door until I felt us jolting rhythmically across the wooden planks of the wharf. When I opened my eyes, it was as though I was seeing things for the first, not the last time. Everything was lit with a pink glow and there was a magic softness in the air, like sinking into a warm bath.

Max walked slowly down the trawler's gangway and kissed Mum roughly on the cheek. He called out to a crewman, 'Solomon, kisim speedboat i-come.' He turned back to Mum. 'I'll come with you in the boat, but I don't trust myself to drive.'

After Solomon had guided each of us into the speedboat, he jumped in and started the engine. Its roar reminded me so strongly of my father I could almost see him sitting there in the shadows at the back of the boat.

We set a course directly out to the twin islands. The trip only took about five minutes, but by the time the boat ran up on the beach, night was falling and everything had a fuzzy outline.

Solomon held a lantern aloft as Max stood in the water and steadied each of us as we stepped out onto the sand. Then he held the lantern high and led us up the beach to the point where the passage between the islands was narrowest.

We gathered around my mother, silently waiting until Max cleared his throat and began.

'God, we commend to you the soul of Bill Cleary, who died in the service of the country he loved. Keep him near to you, we ask this in your name, Amen.'

We all joined in the Amen and Mum stepped forward and shook something over the gentle waves. I dipped my fingers into the tepid water and felt the drag of the rip as it pulled through the channel and out to the black sea. Just like that he was gone.

On the trip back Max sat in the bow with the lantern, lending the boat a ghostly glow. As we approached the lights of the wharf, a silhouette was just visible standing at the end. There was something so otherworldly about his appearance, about the whole evening, that at first I was afraid to ask if the others saw him too. When I summoned the courage to ask if it was Eugene, Max replied, 'Ja.'

As we got close enough to see his outline clearly, Eugene lifted his arm to his cap in a salute. He wasn't saluting us though; he was looking at something over our heads, out in the open sea.

The knock next morning was short, sharp and official. Nathan stood on the other side of the fly wire. 'I'm sorry to bother you so early, but I've got something to show you.'

We led him into the lounge room where he perched awkwardly on my father's armchair.

'It won't be officially released until after the inquest, but I thought you should see it now.'

He handed Susan an envelope. She ripped it open and her eyes went backwards and forwards down the two pages, before she flicked back to the first.

'I'm not sure I understand what it means.' She held it out to me.

I skimmed the first page and phrases like 'cause of death' and 'point of entry' and 'fatal wound' didn't hurt like I thought they would. Until I read *A piece of animal bone measuring 4.2 cm is lodged at the base of the wound, in the lower right ventricle. Indications are that this is the tip of the murder weapon broken off by the force of the impact.*

Relief washed over me. Errol's knife hadn't killed my father.

*The anthropologist, Dr Rudi Andersen, expert on New Ireland customs, confirmed that the bone was the type used to construct ritual weapons on Keriva Island.*

I thought back to our visit to Rudi's island. He must have realised that Tobias was implicated; the old man was the only one allowed to touch the island's ritual objects.

Had my father heard the bending of a twig, a flash of movement out of the corner of his eye before the sharp bone had made him gasp? He hadn't turned; that was clear from the words 'rear entry wound'. But I was tormented by the thought that Dad may have been aware of the betrayal a split second before he felt the blow.

'Billie, you're so pale.'

I turned to Nathan. '*You* understand what it means, don't you? Errol's knife wasn't the murder weapon. A sacred object was used and Tobias was the keeper of all the sacred objects. It *must* have been him.'

He nodded. 'The boy's been released and I'm on my way to arrest the old man. But his guilt may be difficult to prove without witnesses.'

'Nobody will speak against a sangguma?'

'I'm afraid that might be true.'

There was a bitter edge to his voice, and I noticed his eyes, usually chalk white against his inky skin, were bloodshot.

'Thanks for bringing it to us anyway,' Susan said.

Nathan's lip twisted. 'Your father taught me some things are more important than rules.'

# Chapter 29

## Going finish

Susan picked up the report. 'Mum doesn't need to know about any of this until the autopsy becomes official, right? We're booked on tomorrow's plane.'

'Where are we going?'

'The grandparents telegrammed.'

I had a vague memory of a tall white-haired man and a bird-like woman with an Irish accent. We used to visit them at their red-brick pub in Coogee but we hadn't been there for years. That last visit, I'd been basking in the sunshine, sipping red lemonade when my father had yanked me up. 'We're off,' he'd said, and the anger in his voice made me swallow my protest. The old woman followed us, shouting, 'Go back to her then and take your little heathen with you.'

I didn't know what the word meant but I knew she had called me a bad thing.

And now it seemed like we were going to have to depend on people that had called us a bad name, who didn't bother sending us a Christmas Mass card because they thought we were going to hell anyway. I couldn't stop my tears.

Susan squeezed my hand. 'I know it's hard. But we've got to get Mum away from this place.'

Later she opened my bedroom door and slid a suitcase across the floor. I tried to pretend I was just going back to school, like I did at the end of every holiday, but tears kept falling as I wrapped special keepsakes, like shells and beads, in cotton wool.

I avoided looking in the mirror for the rest of the day, waiting for the cover of darkness to venture out. At dusk, I found my sisters sitting at the kitchen table with the Negrita bottle.

I nodded outside. 'I have to say goodbye.'

Susan waved her hand. 'Go.'

My heart was thumping as I walked through the shadows of Chinatown. I had to tell Desmond we were leaving but the Wu Emporium stood in darkness. I knocked on the door but the only sound was the bark of a distant dog. I should have known where he actually lived but I didn't, so all I could do was head for Lucille's.

The tangerine Moke was parked out the front of the house but to my surprise Errol's mother, May, opened the door and stood blinking in the porch light.

'They're not here,' she mumbled.

'Isn't it great news about Errol?'

'Yes. They all at Mr Chan's for big party.'

'Why aren't *you* there?'

'He say better me not go.'

'Cedric?'

'My boy.'

'Errol? But he's so proud of you.'

'Mr Chan been teaching my boy 'bout politics.'

'Oh, May, I'm sorry.'

'It's okay. Mr Chan, he big man *now*, but my boy, he gonna be *bigger*.' She patted my hand. 'You go, now, to Mr Chan's.'

I couldn't stop thinking about the encounter as I walked along in the dark, trying to retrace the route to Cedric's. The Errol I thought I knew would never shame his mother like that. I wondered if the things Cedric had been teaching Errol involved Dad? What kind of reception would I get at the party? There'd been no love lost between Cedric and my father and here I was walking straight into the lion's den.

The sounds of a party rang out as I walked down Cedric's driveway. The front door was wide open and a beam of light picked out Errol's car and a dozen others parked at all angles.

I could hear a man slurring along to Bob Marley, hamming up the Jamaican accent and laughing as he shouted about shooting the sheriff.

I stepped inside slowly, expecting to be challenged, but the people in the hallway didn't notice me. More people were standing around holding beers in what looked like a kitchen, and figures were dancing in a room beyond. There were a lot of middle-aged local men in shorts and shirts and young girls in shiny dresses. I didn't recognise anyone, until Cedric lurched into the hall, his arm around Errol.

Errol saw me first. 'Billie. You heard then.'

His eyes were flat. No pleasure to see me, no gratitude for helping to get him out. Just a flicker of guilty surprise.

Cedric looked startled. 'No hard feelings then, Miss Cleary?'

I shook my head.

He tossed his head. 'But why would there be? Your father thought he knew this country and its people, but he was wrong.'

'I *tried* to warn him, Billie.' Errol stepped closer to me and I felt the old magnetic pull.

'He wouldn't even listen to his own daughter. How was I supposed to make him listen to me?'

Cedric chuckled. 'Well said, my boy.'

Errol looked as though he'd been waiting his whole life to hear those words.

It was nauseating. I turned and walked back into the dark as Errol called after me.

'Let her go, son,' Cedric shouted. 'Plenty of willing girls right here.'

The heavy door closed with a thud. I waited to see if Errol would come after me but he didn't. Once again, I'd wasted precious time on him when I should have been trying to find Desmond, and now suddenly it was all too late.

The bush seemed to close around me as I stumbled homeward. Vines twisted into strange silhouettes and flying foxes squealed overhead but it was a comfort to be cloaked in its darkness. The lights of home loomed ahead as I approached. I hadn't noticed the parked car until I drew abreast, and Desmond stepped out of it.

I moved towards him, touched his arm to check he was really there. 'I went to the shop but when you weren't there, I didn't know where to find you.'

'You must have just missed me. I've been parked here a while now.'

'Then I went to the party at Cedric's, hoping you'd be there.'

'Not likely.'

'I've been an idiot, haven't I?'

He ran his hand down my face. 'It's going to be okay, Billie.'

'But there's no more time. We fly out in the morning.'

'Where are you going?'

'My grandparents' pub in Coogee. It sounds mad but I can't think of the name – my dad had a big bust-up with them and we haven't been since I was about five. It's an Irish name …'

'Not Cleary's?'

'No, prettier than that … Rose of Tralee! That's it.'

His face shone in the moonlight. He put his arms around me and I wanted to stay like that forever.

A cough came from the house. Susan was standing just inside the front door.

'I suppose I better go,' I whispered.

'I'll write. The Rose of Tralee Hotel, Coogee.'

Our lips clung together until another cough made me reluctantly pull away.

'I'm sorry,' Susan said, as I sidled inside. 'But you've got to be up in a few hours.'

When she woke me in the half-light, I thought of the last time I'd got up early to catch a plane. Only five weeks had passed but it felt like a lifetime. Back then, I couldn't have imagined anything could feel worse than going back to school, waking with a sick feeling in your stomach but having to put on a brave face for your parents.

That morning we were all putting on a brave face. Mum presented her sewing machine to Suriwan and Dad's watch to Tahl, and even Rosie only broke for a moment. I thought we might all falter when Julius appeared in his new chauffeur's cap to drive us to the airport, but Mum was firm as she passed him an envelope.

Our airport send-off was an anti-climax. Only the Commissioner, Nathan and Martha were waiting next to the gate.

The Commissioner held out two rolled-up flags. 'I'm sorry, I forgot these at the funeral, with all the kerfuffle.'

Mum's hands were full with her beauty case so I took them and clutched them to my chest. What a relief when the pilots announced it was time to board. The airline agent stammered his condolences and we dragged ourselves across the tarmac. Lingering at the top of the stairway, I took one last gulp of the warm salty air of home.

# Chapter 30



The trip from Brisbane to Port Moresby passes quicker than I remember it. Rosie drones on about how dreadful she was to me back in the old days and how she wants to make amends, until I close my eyes and pretend to be asleep. I picture myself back in Kavieng, floating in the channel between the islands, lifted on the gentle tide. I must drift off to sleep because before I know it Susan is whispering to wake up and the seatbelt sign has pinged on.

As the plane circles for its final descent, I look down on the villages clinging to the water's edge by their stilts. The dusty hills behind the sprawl look parched and I long for Kavieng's green palms.

'God, you forget that heat, don't you?' Susan gasps as we struggle across the tarmac.

She's right. The heat is physical, like an animal to be wrestled each day. By the time we reach the shade of the terminal, my underarms are damp with sweat.

Errol had offered to send an official car to collect us from the airport but I'd wanted to keep some independence. I'm doubting the wisdom of that decision as a group of eager taxi drivers mill around us.

Susan picks the eldest, a man who looks about as old as my father would have been. He grins, revealing teeth unstained by the betel nut red characteristic of most of the others.

Trying our rusty Pidgin, we discover the driver is from Madang, Port Moresby's a bad place and things had been better in the *taim bilong masta*. This is no doubt why Susan chose an older man. People of his vintage are a comforting bridge to the past; he'll tell us what we want to hear, whether it's the truth or not.

I am struck by the thought that Errol is going to look older, nothing like the sullen youths lolling beside the road the whole way into town, like a menacing guard of honour.

Susan pays the taxi driver with a handful of kina notes.

The hotel is one we stayed at with our parents, spruced up for the ten-year anniversary with fresh white paintwork and a bowl of hibiscus at the reception desk. The local man behind the desk in patterned shirt and baggy pants looks like Lionel Ritchie; he's friendly and meets our eyes in a way he never would have in the old days. When Susan checks in, he hands her an officially embossed envelope.

We've booked a family room so none of us have to sleep alone. Despite the razor wire on top of the perimeter fence, or perhaps because of it, we're all nervous about security, which isn't helped by a sign on the wall outlining the conditions of the current State of Emergency, including a midnight curfew.

The desk clerk nods towards it. 'Don't worry too much about that – it's mainly for the raskols, so they don't mess up the celebrations.'

'Who are the raskols?' Rosie asks.

'They live in shantytowns. Maybe they try to get work when they first come, but now they just make trouble.' He lowers his voice, 'Most of them are Highlanders. Can't hold their alcohol.'

We exchange nervous smiles.

Our room smells of wet air, and the air conditioner is on a glacial setting. There's a queen bed and a single, which

Rosie immediately puts her bags on. Looks like Susan and I are sharing.

'What's in the envelope?' Rosie asks.

Susan reads out an invitation to be the guests of Errol Chan, Honourable Member for New Ireland, at a dinner at the Papua Yacht Club.

'Well, it's not *us* he wants to see, is it?' Rosie says.

'She's right,' Susan says. 'I'm happy to support you at the ceremony, but … you're on your own with this one.'

I've spent as long as Rosie normally does getting dressed, trying different clothing combinations to get my message just right. Attractive not sexy, sensible not boring, appealing not available. The dress I've chosen is possibly a little skimpy but the evening's still damn hot.

Out the taxi window, twilight has thrown a flattering peach glow over Moresby's tawdry face. The sights and sounds of the dusk, the distant barking of dogs, the smell of campfires and the buzzing of mosquitos reminds me of Kavieng.

It's hard to believe how much I once trusted Errol. I cringe when I remember how vulnerable I'd been, letting him drive me to Keriva and take me to the far side of the island. I'm still not sure whether he can be trusted but I can look after myself a lot better these days.

He's waiting alone out the front of the yacht club, no minions in sight. I recognise him from a distance, the definition of his chest under the shirt, his rugby back's slender hips and compactness. Funny, I'd never thought of him as short, but he isn't tall. His face is hidden under a sweeping Dustin Hoffman-like fringe, and I take in the well-cut shirt, pleated pants and boat shoes.

He holds out his hand and when I take it, he squeezes mine with his other hand like he's been to some kind of diplomatic charm school.

The yacht club has all the trappings you'd find anywhere in the world – well-upholstered furniture, ice buckets and stunning harbour views. I don't really look at Errol until we're seated at a table by the window, and when I do, his eyes are tired.

A waiter appears with two flutes of champagne, then glides away.

'Cheers,' Errol says, as we clink glasses. 'How does it feel to be back?'

'I think I'm a bit nervous.'

'About?'

'I don't know. Meeting you again, maybe, just being back in this country.'

'Does it still feel like home?'

'This town was never home; *Kavieng* was home. I've thought about going back there so many times but I think I'd rather keep it the way it is in my dreams.'

'You still dream about it?'

I nod.

Errol shifts in his seat. 'How's Desmond?'

'Great. Really great.'

'I'm sorry we lost touch. He was the best friend I ever had.'

'He's *my* best friend now.'

He leans back, self-satisfied. 'I'm really pleased you got together in the end, you know.'

'How's Vanessa?'

He shakes his head. 'What, you thought me and Vanessa …?'

'You were pretty intense back then. Made me feel really juvenile.'

'I never saw her after I was released. No letter, nothing. I was pretty cut up about it – even wrote to her school, but they sent it back. Reckon she's probably shacked up with some rich old guy.'

'But you've got somebody?'

'I'm married, yes.'

'Who is she?'

I'd swear he looked embarrassed if I didn't know better. 'She's young.'

'A local girl?'

'Yes, she's from Kavieng, a niece of someone who owes Cedric. Or Cedric owes, I can never quite remember which.' He takes a swig of champagne. 'Young and sweet but so naïve.'

I don't want to think about how naïve I'd once been. 'How's your mother?'

'Pleased I married a local girl. Of course it goes down well with the voters too.'

A canoe, lit up by a hurricane lamp hanging from its mast, crosses the inky water outside our window.

'Do you still catch sharks?'

He laughs. 'There's enough of them in this town, ay? But seriously, not anymore. When I go back, everyone wants to shake my hand and talk business. I don't get the chance to relax, let alone go out in my canoe.'

'So, you regret following in Cedric's footsteps?'

'I regret some things. Lucille and I don't really talk anymore; I regret that. But don't feel too sorry for me.'

'No?'

He leans back. 'It's been an easy road. Walked straight

onto the council, then pretty much got handed my seat when Cedric moved on to greener pastures. Word is I'll be in the next Cabinet. That's why I'm in the position to do something for your father. And for you.'

'If you really want to do something for me, you could lock up Tobias.'

His voice drops. 'The old fellow keeled over just after independence. Like he saw the writing on the wall.'

'What? He's really dead?'

'Nobody told you? I thought Nathan would have.'

I've gone cold all over. I sit, trying to gather my thoughts.

'It's the first of these honours we've given, you know ...' Errol pauses like he's waiting for my thanks.

An old, confused anger is growing inside me. 'I didn't come all this way just to pick up an award, you know. I need to know what it means.'

'It's to acknowledge his sacrifice ...'

'Don't bullshit me, Errol. I want to know why you're doing this – you never even liked him. Is it to ease your guilt?'

He flinches. 'Maybe in some ways it is. You were always so innocent, Billie, you made me feel bad. Even when I wasn't doing anything, I felt bad for my thoughts. Your dad was the same. I could see straight through him, and I felt bad even while I was taking advantage of him.'

'What are you saying?'

'It's been on my conscience.'

The champagne churns in my stomach. '*What's* been on your conscience? What exactly happened that night?'

He takes a deep breath. 'Your father found me near my hut and humiliated me in front of my boys, the way he enjoyed doing. Warned me about touching white girls, treated me like a pervert.' Tears of frustration spring into his eyes.

He's not a hardened politician anymore, he's a wounded boy. If he's acting, he's doing an amazing job.

He takes another deep breath and this one seems to catch in his throat. 'So, you see, it was like a reflex action.'

'*What* was like a reflex action?'

He puts his face in his hand.

I pull his hand away. 'Look at me, damn it.'

My voice is barely a hiss but other diners are staring at us and the waiter looks over, alarmed. We sit in silence until the conversations gradually resume.

Then Errol speaks quietly, 'At the time, it made perfect sense.'

'What? What did you *do*?'

'Nothing. I did nothing. That's the point. I didn't lift a finger.'

'What do you mean?'

'When I was heading out ...'

'To meet Vanessa?'

He nods. 'I saw your father going into the bush with Tobias, right near the spirit house. Something about it didn't look right, but I was so angry with your father, I thought, let him look after himself.'

A wave of relief rushes through me. 'So, all you did was turn a blind eye? Why didn't you say so?'

'I tried at first but the police wouldn't listen, and when I saw you at the wharf ... I just couldn't bring myself to talk about that night.'

'When he warned you to keep away ... from white girls ... was he was talking about me?'

He shakes his head. 'No, no, it was all about Vanessa. He knew about her and me.'

So, Dad had been protecting Vanessa, not me.

He's staring at me. 'Is that what you've been thinking all these years, that it was about you?'

'I didn't know what to think. That last time I saw you with Cedric, you acted kind of guilty.'

Errol clicks his fingers, and the hovering waiter refills our glasses. I notice it's French champagne.

He takes a gulp before he speaks. 'I *was* feeling guilty that night at Cedric's. Going to prison had boosted my popularity out of sight. People treated me like a folk hero – and it felt like it was because of what happened to your father.'

'So, this is about forgiveness?'

'In a way. I rang your place in Coff's before I sent you the invitation, you know. Desmond answered.'

'He never mentioned it.'

'He said you still blame yourself for what happened.' He takes my hand in a strong, warm grip. 'You were a kid back then, Billie, the adults were in charge. It *wasn't* your fault. It's time to forgive yourself.'

# Chapter 31

## Disco

It's a spur-of-the-moment thing. As Errol's official car pulls into my hotel driveway, its high beams light up a banner above the entrance: *'Party like it's 1975 at the Firehouse – where there's smoke, there's disco!'*

Errol turns to me. 'How about a night cap?'

I look at my watch. 'Isn't it curfew now?'

He laughs. 'Curfew doesn't apply to people like us. Besides, this is your hotel, remember?'

'Maybe just the one.'

It's against my better judgement. I want to be fresh to face the ceremony tomorrow, and I imagine Dad whispering in my ear that nothing good ever happens after midnight. But I haven't been able to talk about my father and the night he died with anyone. Even Desmond stiffens at the mention of his name and treads so carefully around anything to do with that time, as though he's afraid my heart might break all over again.

Not that there's much chance of talking in the bar Errol steers me into. It has small candlelit tables and a cosy atmosphere but it's right next to the disco and the music is pumping.

The barman puts a bottle of Scotch and two glasses on the table, and I'm guessing Errol's been here before. Errol clinks his glass against mine and grins. He throws his drink down and I follow. I'm not used to hard liquor and it burns my throat.

The music sits between us like a wall of sound. We try to shout over Tears for Fears and Madonna, but there's no point. Errol gets up and has a word to the barman, who goes across and swings the door closed. The music drops to a dull hum. The barman moves to the end of the bar and stands with his back to us, cleaning glasses.

'That's better.' Errol leans forward. 'Don't be fooled by that fellow over there in the corner. He's listening to every word.'

'Why?'

'Cedric has spies everywhere. He likes to keep tabs on me, who I'm talking to, who I'm close to.'

'But I thought you and Cedric were good now ...'

'You thought we were buddies, is that what you mean? Because I'm like him?' Errol refills our glasses and takes another swig. 'I'm nothing like him, *nothing*. If he was bad before, he's so much worse now. Australia still pays for half of everything in Moresby, but nobody's keeping tabs on it except the sandal brigade, consultants from down south who have their snouts in the trough as well.'

Errol's eyes are flashing; he's getting worked up, the way he used to. 'I hate the way he skims money off the top – we argue about it all the time. But because I asked him for help the *one* time I was desperate ... you know how desperate I must have been to do that, Billie, don't you? Because of that, he acts like he owns me now, and everyone else acts like he owns me too. Even *you* ...'

He looks so deeply sad that I want to reach out and comfort him but I'm afraid of falling under his spell again.

'I'm sorry, I'm out of touch with all of that. I'm a bit less clueless about everything, though, now I run a business.'

'What kind of business?'

'Horticultural.'

'What cultural?'

'Horticulture – you know, plants and stuff.'

'I don't remember you being interested in plants.'

'I wasn't but there was a plant nursery at the end of our street in Sydney. I got a part-time job there and loved it so much I did a course when I left school. My specialty's the tropical plants – hibiscus, frangipani, the canna lilies. One day I remembered my dad used to talk about going to Coff's Harbour, so I thought I'd try it for six months. The minute I walked out into that balmy climate and saw the rich soil it was like I'd come home.'

'And how does Desmond fit into the picture?'

'He tracked me down. After we went finish, we started living at our grandparents' pub in Coogee, but Mum had a falling out with them almost straight away and we moved every few months for a year or two. Desmond had written to the pub and the letter finally caught up with me. We started writing to each other and one day he just stepped off the bus in Coff's and told me he'd left his accounting course.'

'Accounting?' Errol shakes his head.

'I know. You've seen his sketches, right? He's an artist.'

'So, what does he do now?'

'He's a landscape designer. We run the business together – he does the plans and the structural work and I'm in charge of the plants.' I pull a photo from my wallet and pass it across. 'We built it all together – the house, the sheds, the pond. I know it sounds corny, but it's our little piece of paradise.'

'It doesn't sound corny, it sounds … nice.'

He's looking at me with something like envy. 'I knew Desmond loved you, you know, right from the beginning. That night I introduced you outside the Imperial picture theatre.'

'No. Really?'

'Oh yeah. Smitten from the moment he laid eyes on you.'

'You didn't let on …'

'I was a prick back then, what can I say?'

I'm suddenly dead tired. 'I'm sorry, Errol, but I need to get myself to bed. It's a big day tomorrow.'

He lays his hand on my thigh. 'You're not going to dance with me?'

I shake my head. 'You know, when I first got your letter, I really didn't know what to make of it.'

His eyes twinkle. 'I bet you thought it might be a ploy to get you into bed finally?'

I nod.

He leans closer. 'Would that be such a bad idea?'

'Oh, yes.' I roll my eyes. 'It so would.'

We share a laugh.

'Are you going to be okay?' I ask.

He nods towards his glass. 'Don't worry, I'm used to it.

Can't sleep without at least a couple under my belt.'

'I didn't mean the drink. It's just, well you seem a bit … sad?'

He shakes his head. 'No, no, I'm fine. Actually, I might head into the disco, find some company.'

He makes a feeble attempt at a playboy grin. I reach out and take his hand. Bugger the barman.

'Thank you,' I say. 'For everything.'

# Chapter 32

## The ceremony

The breakfast smorgasbord is better than I was expecting; the tropical fruits of our childhood laid out on platters beside the cornflakes and toast. I take a slice of pawpaw.

Back at the table, Rosie's gushing. 'Someone in the breakfast line said Bob Hawke's in town. Maybe we'll get to meet him?'

Susan rolls her eyes. 'He's hardly going to be at *Dad's* thing, is he? He's here for the main event, not a sideshow. Sorry, that came out wrong … but you know what I mean?'

'Who *will* be there then?' I ask.

'I really have no idea, but if we're going to be on time you'd better drink up that coffee. It's already twenty to eight.'

I gulp down the last mouthful of pawpaw.

Susan shepherds us out to the front of the hotel, where the official car is waiting. It's the standard white Statesman with bird of paradise flags fluttering, driven by the same man who dropped me off the night before and presumably delivered Errol home after whatever he got up to.

We all slide into the back seat and it's like we're sitting behind Julius again. The driver's even wearing the same kind of peaked cap.

Once we're under way, Rosie turns to me and grins. 'You look a bit hungover, Billie.'

'You should see the other guy.'

'We're about to, aren't we?' Susan allows herself a chuckle.

'What did Lover Boy have to say for himself?' Rosie asks.

The driver's head inclines just enough to show he's listening.

'When are you going to grow up, Rosie?'

Susan squeezes my hand. 'Come on, she didn't mean any harm. We're all a bit wound up. All this ... well, it brings it back, doesn't it?'

The greenery outside the car window looks manicured and artfully punctuated by orange and purple flashes of hibiscus and bougainvillea. A pair of green gates topped by a giant golden bird of paradise crest loom, with a sign declaring 'National Parliament'.

The gates swing open and we're waved through by an army sergeant in the sentry box. The driveway snakes around trimmed hedges beside a lake until a spectacular pyramid appears ahead. It looks like the *haus tambarans* I remember from Dad's books on Melanesian spirit worship, but ten times the size. It's a beautiful sight.

A huge mosaic set into the triangular façade looms over us. An orange sun reigns over a world of aqua rivers and brown men, pigs and cassowaries, emerald crocodiles and fish.

'This place is amazing,' Rosie whispers.

'The news cameras didn't do it justice,' Susan says.

I remember the fleeting footage of Prince Charles cutting a ribbon.

An army officer waits for us at the top of the stairs. I dawdle after my sisters, savouring the cool morning air, the solemn expression of the sentry, everything about this magical place, presided over by that mesmerising mosaic world. Even the doors are mysterious, set into a circular frame like the entrance to a hobbit hole, their handles a pair of kundu drums. When they swing open, we step into a cavernous entrance hall.

A dapper young local man in a suit coughs. 'Please follow me.'

He walks us towards the far end of the hall and as we approach a small dais emerges in front of several rows of chairs. A large photo of my father in a khaki shirt on an easel makes a lump swell in my throat.

We are ushered into the front row and I see some familiar faces. The old Commissioner is there in civilian clothes, so I'm guessing he's retired. A Papuan in a Commissioner's uniform must be the current incumbent. Nathan is here too, grey around the temples and heavier around the middle. He leans forward and nods to us. I'm disappointed Martha's not with him but relieved there's no sign of Cedric.

The crowd murmurs and suddenly Errol is standing on the dais, handsome in an expensive cream suit and shower-slick hair. His eyes are sharp and as he clears his throat to speak, I know it's going to be okay.

'When Bill Cleary first came to this country in 1953, the kiap was in charge of everything. He supervised road and bridge building, took the census and kept the peace. He was an engineer, public servant, policeman – even magistrate. Many of the older kiaps found such power hard to give up. But twenty years later, Bill was on the brink of handing it all over to one of my countrymen.' He acknowledges Nathan with a nod. 'Bill Cleary and I had our differences.' He takes a deep breath. 'But when he was tragically murdered in January 1974, he died in the service of this country. It was precisely *because* he recognised that our time had come that a madman struck him down.'

He holds up a shiny silver disc in a black box. 'We are indeed fortunate to have Bill Cleary's three daughters with us here today, to receive this medal, on the day we commemorate the tenth year of our nationhood.' He beckons to us and I'm the first to stumble forward.

After the intimacy of our meeting last night, this formality feels artificial, like we're pretending to be strangers in front of the crowd. When he shakes my hand, he's Errol the politician, with the loose grip and the flat eyes. I like to think I'm older and wiser but he's still as elusive as ever.

Errol's moved on, shaking Rosie's hand before presenting the box to Susan. We stand beside him, then Susan raises the box and there's a smattering of polite applause. We pose for the photographer who has stepped forward and, in a flash, it's over. The people in the seats stand and begin to disperse.

Errol points to a linen-covered table set with an urn and rows of white cups and saucers. 'Shall we?'

He seems ill at ease with my sisters.

Susan turns to him as she takes a cup. 'Your words meant a lot ...'

'Thank you. It took me some time to put my thoughts together. It feels like such a long time ago, but at the same time like yesterday.'

As Nathan approaches my sisters, Errol retreats to the space beside me.

'I miss Eugene,' I say, almost to myself.

'Eugene?'

'You know, Dad's sergeant. I don't know why, but I thought he might be here.'

The last sentence hangs awkwardly in the air, like a criticism.

Errol cocks his head. 'I always wondered why that fella didn't speak up for me.'

'Which fellow? Eugene?'

He nods.

'What do you mean speak up?'

'Well, he could have said your father was alive and well when I left the island. It would have given me an alibi, saved a lot of grief.'

I shake my head. 'But he wasn't with Dad. He stayed with the boat until it was dark.'

Errol touches my arm, as though to soften the impact of his words. 'Look, I don't know what he told you, but I know what I saw with my own eyes. The sergeant was with your father when he went into the bush with Tobias.'

# Chapter 33

## Celebrations

Errol's frowning at me. 'Are you okay?'

'Just feel a bit faint.'

'I'm sorry if this has upset you. I was trying to make things better.'

'No, it's been good, honestly. It's just …'

'You didn't know about the sergeant being there?'

I shake my head.

The aide suddenly appears at Errol's side.

'I'm afraid it's time for me to go.' Errol squeezes my hand. He sounds reluctant but he's out the door before I have time to open my mouth.

The aide escorts us back to the entrance. We pause on the other side of the door.

'Wow, that was a bit of a whirlwind.'

'I thought he did a really good job,' Susan says.

We slide back into the car's cool cabin.

Rosie pops her head over the front seat. 'When does the big celebration kick off?'

The driver frowns. 'Kick off?'

'When does it start?'

'Flag ceremony is at sunset, big stadium on harbour. But Prime Minister inspecting soldiers before that. And there will be many people. I pick you up at four.'

Fate has handed me the missing piece in Dad's story – Eugene lied. All I've got to do is go to Kavieng and track him down. I'm going to keep my new travel plans to myself, at least until the celebrations are over. If my sisters find out now, they'll try to stop me.

'I might pop into town and pick up a souvenir for Desmond,' I say.

'Is it safe in town?' Susan asks.

'Don't worry. I'll take a taxi and pay him to wait for me.'

'No taxi, miss,' the driver says. 'Mr Chan tell me to look out for you. *I* take you past town now.'

In the town centre there's a scattering of high-rise buildings and even a traffic light. The schools must be closed for the celebrations because there are children everywhere, holding balloons and eating ice creams.

I head straight for the Air Niugini office and buy a ticket on tomorrow's flight to Kavieng. On the way back to the car, I pass a young girl selling commemorative t-shirts and buy one in Desmond's size.

After lunch, we head back to our room. Rosie and I flop down on the beds as Susan turns on the air conditioner. 'Remember how Mum and Dad made us have a rest after lunch when we were little?'

'We used to hate it,' Rosie says. '*Now* look at us.'

Susan sits on my side of the bed. 'Are you all right, Billie? You've hardly said a word since this morning.'

'I guess it's just hit me.'

'What has?'

'How strange it is being here … without him.'

Susan strokes my hair as she settles next to me. 'We all feel it, don't we, Rosie?'

Rosie murmurs assent and we lapse into a communal silence.

We're woken by a loud rapping on the door. We jump up, splash water on our faces and throw on fresh dresses.

As the car turns onto the highway, it looks like every single citizen, from the babes slung in *bilums* on their mothers' backs to the oldest *lapun* hobbling on walking sticks, is on the road in front of us.

Rosie groans. 'We're going to miss it all if we can't get around this crowd. We could walk faster than this!'

'Yes, but without this lovely air conditioner, you'd be soaked in a minute,' Susan says. 'Besides, you might not be safe out there.'

She's right; there are a lot of young men running along next to the car, chanting with excitement. Every so often some of them bang on our windows until the driver sounds a warning blast.

Bright hand-painted billboards adorned with slogans of celebration appear on the roadside. '*Rothmans is proud to walk into the future with a strong young nation,*' reads one and, '*Welcom Mr Bob Hawke, friend bilong Gof Witlem*' another. The billboards are fringed with garlands of frangipani and hibiscus, so many that it seems impossible any flowers could be left on a tree.

'Susan's right, you know,' I say. 'We may as well just sit back and let Julius here worry about getting us there.'

The driver turns around in puzzlement. 'My name not Julius, Miss. It's Linus.'

'I'm sorry, Linus. You remind me of a driver called Julius back in Kavieng. He was … very special to us.'

'You live in Kavieng?' Linus grins.

'Until 1974.'

He taps his chest. 'Me New Ireland man.'

'So, you and Errol are wantoks?'

He nods. 'My village just down the road from Keriva.'

The car keeps edging forward until the stadium looms ahead above the crowd. Some of the people running alongside peel off and head towards an open set of cyclone-wire gates.

As we near the stadium, uniforms are suddenly everywhere. Policemen line the perimeter and soldiers in jungle-green berets are thick around the entrance. The car in front of ours lets out its passengers, a Fijian in traditional skirt and a white man in a suit.

Linus pulls up beside a bamboo shelter. 'This VIP entrance. I'll pick you up here after big salute.'

'Salute?' I ask, but a soldier has already opened the door and is beckoning us out into the heat.

The army cordon valiantly tries to keep the line of dignitaries separate from the crowd surging around us. The rising smell of pig grease and sweat reminds me of sports days of old.

A young Papuan with a clipboard stands at the bottom of the stairs, checking off names as we are ushered upwards.

Nathan waves and we take a seat next to him. He looks un-comfortable and sweaty in a suit and tie. There's still no sign of his wife.

'How's Martha?' I ask.

He frowns. 'She went back to the village a few years ago. She couldn't get used to Moresby.'

'I'm sorry.'

He lifts his shoulders. 'I'm in charge of provincial government now, you see, so I have to stay here.'

'Dad always said you'd do well.'

I see movement out of the corner of my eye and there's Errol sitting further down our row, finger raised in greeting. Beside him, staring straight ahead, is a young woman, who I'm guessing is his wife. The set of her shoulders suggests she's trying not to look at whoever her husband's waving at.

She's not much older than twenty and her oversized lace collar makes her look like she's playing dress-ups. But she has a kind of radiance that makes her cheeks gleam, just like May's used to.

Down below us a brass band starts up as soldiers march up and down the oval. On the opposite side the crowd is spilling over the picket fence, with some clinging to the towering side barriers or hanging from trees at the back. Polite applause from the stand is drowned out by wild whoops and cheers from the surrounding crowd.

Susan leans towards Nathan. 'Will this finish soon, do you think?'

The afternoon has droned on with speech and counter-speech from most of the local and imported dignitaries and now darkness has fallen like a dropped curtain.

'We're waiting for the gun salute – that's when we stuffed shirts are allowed to leave.'

Errol's wife is pushing along the row past Nathan and my sisters. As she passes, she touches my arm and nods towards the aisle. I follow, intrigued.

We hover in the shadows.

'You're Errol's wife?'

She nods. 'I'm Penelope. And you're the woman who has something on my husband.'

'What do you mean?'

She's vibrating with silent intensity. 'He's hardly slept since he sent you that letter.'

I shake my head. 'I don't have anything on him, I swear. I guess I remind him of painful things … from the past. But don't worry, I'm leaving tomorrow. I'll be out of your lives forever.'

Her reply is lost in an ear-shattering boom. A cloud of smoke rises from the direction of the harbour. The big guns ring out. *Bang – bang – bang.* The sounds echo in my chest like an explosion of emotion.

As the final bang dies away, the brass band begins the mournful strains of 'Auld Lang Syne'. It feels like a personal message, a recognition of our past, my father's as well as the country's. But it's not my country anymore.

# Chapter 34

## Kavieng

'What do you mean you're not coming home with us?' Rosie turns from the mirror, lipstick pointed.

'We're not leaving you alone in this place.' Susan sounds equally fierce.

'I won't be here, that's the thing.' I try to sound calm and sensible. 'I'm flying to Kavieng at lunchtime.'

'Why go back there?'

'I need to find Eugene. Dad's old policeman, remember? Errol said something that made me think Eugene didn't tell the truth back then.'

'It's a bit last minute, isn't it?' Rosie says. 'What are we supposed to tell Desmond?'

'I've already told him.'

I'd left a message on the answering machine but I didn't need to tell them that.

'Isn't Rabaul about to blow?'

'That was a false alarm. The volcano's quietened down, honestly.'

'You're going all that way in the hope of catching up with some old policeman? How do you even know he's still alive?' Rosie says.

'He's not that old. I know I may not find him, but I've got to know I've done everything I can to try.'

'We're not going to change your mind, are we?' Susan turns to Rosie. 'We never could, when she was like this.'

I hand the medal box to Susan. 'Keep this safe, will you?'

She looks like she's going to cry. 'Keep yourself safe too, little sister.'

It's only as the Fokker Friendship banks over the Bismarck Sea, minutes from landing in Kavieng, that I realise how rash I've been. My decision not to involve Errol or my sisters in my plans means I'm entirely on my own. I haven't a clue where to start. Where to stay, where to eat, how to find Eugene? Maybe I should have started my search in Rabaul? As these questions fly around in my head, I can't seem to get enough air into my lungs.

The young boy next to me nudges my arm. 'Are you okay, miss?'

His mother, who has the stature and grace of a New Irelander, takes one look at me and pushes the call button.

The air hostess kneels at my side. 'Hold your breath for five and then breathe out slowly.'

Stop making a scene, I tell myself, as she counts to five. I imagine the whole cabin is watching, but when I look up, they all seem to be busy stowing things away for landing.

'Do you feel better?' the hostess asks.

I nod.

'Good,' she says. 'I have to strap in for the landing but just keep up that slow breathing.'

I look out the window and it's all there, laid out like a map. Sea, reef, lines of palms, roads. Exactly like last time. Tears prick my eyes so I screw them closed and brace. Brace, brace … and just when I think we're going to overshoot the runway, a thump and I'm thrown back against my seat.

The plane bumps along the tarmac and past the wire fence where I spent so many afternoons waiting for the afternoon plane. I stay in my seat as the other passengers shuffle off.

The hostess comes back to check on me. 'Not many

tourists make it this far but I'm guessing you're not a tourist?'

'I used to live here, a long time ago.'

'How long?'

'Twelve years.'

'So, you've come back to …?'

'I'm looking for someone. He used to be a policeman.'

'Well, you won't have any trouble finding the police station. I don't think anything's changed in this town in the last twelve years.'

'Where should I stay?'

'The club's the only decent one.'

'Wow, is that place still running?'

'It's under new management.'

I walk down the metal stairs just in front of the crew and drift towards the same little fibro building, which looks even smaller than it used to. My suitcase looks lonely on the metal trailer sitting in front. Most of the cars have left the carpark and there's no sign of a taxi.

'Hey.' The hostess leans out the doorway of a minibus. 'Can we give you a lift into town?'

'Thanks.' I drag my suitcase up the steps and scramble into a seat opposite the driver. He tips his cap.

As we pull out onto the road, a sign in the *malangan* colours of ochre, white and black welcomes us to *Nui Ailan*

*Province.* The road has more potholes than I remember as we bounce past rows of houses on stilts. A sign announces the ten-year anniversary in bold Oceanic style.

The shops need a coat of paint but they're still operating and don't have the security screens found in Port Moresby. The streets are busy; I catch myself searching for a familiar face or anything to anchor my memories to, but there seems no connection between the jumbled scenes in my brain and this town.

Another boldly coloured sign announces The Kavieng Club as the bus turns into the driveway and we pass beneath a wooden arch. I take a deep breath as we pull up in front of the familiar concrete steps where I waited for my sisters so many years ago.

I expected to relax back into these familiar surroundings like I'd never left but I feel dislocated; everything looks similar yet feels foreign. Darkness is falling and the mosquitos are starting to bite so I force myself up the steps. Straight away I see someone has redecorated. The old Chesterfields and armchairs have been replaced with black lacquer tables and hot-pink chairs. There are rock posters on the walls and the bar is framed by fairy lights.

Suddenly the chopstick intro of 'Hong Kong Garden' blares out from a speaker and it's like I'm walking into a nightclub. I can hear a voice above the music, tinkling on the verge of laughter, with a smoker's rasp. It's a voice I recognise.

A spotlight shines on the woman behind the bar, like this is her stage and she's the star. She has short spikey black hair and rockstar eye makeup.

'Lucille?' I shout above the music and the chat.

She looks me up and down before her crimson lips break into a smile. 'Billie? You're all grown up! I *love* your hair long.'

I'm a tongue-tied teenager again, as she rushes forward and pulls me into a familiar patchouli hug.

After a surprisingly good fish curry in the dining room, Lucille leads me into a parlour. She pulls a bottle of vodka and an ice bucket out from behind the bar. I play with my glass as she knocks hers back.

'So, you and Desmond, hey …' she says, in that playful tone I never quite knew how to take.

'Yeah, I know. He came and found me. In the place I'd run away to.'

'Which is?'

'Coff's Harbour. It's on the north coast of New South Wales. Dad talked about going there to fish one day but …'

'He never got the chance.'

'It reminded me so much of this place. Tropical and boats everywhere. So, I stayed.'

'What do you do there?'

'We run a landscape business together.'

'It's funny how you and Desmond seem so obvious now. Much better match than you and Errol.'

'I know, right?' I laugh. 'I like your punk princess look.'

'I'm a big fan. I play them all the time – Sex Pistols, The Clash, and of course the queen of them all, Siouxsie.'

'You know you look just like her.'

She beams.

'And you don't look a day older than last time I saw you.'

'The makeup helps.'

'I wasn't expecting to find you *here*.'

She grins. 'You think the club's too posh for me?'

'I didn't mean that. I just thought you would have gone south. Like Desmond's folks.'

'Errol looked after me. Made sure I got my citizenship, that sort of thing.' She pours herself another slug.

'I guess I always pictured you out there.' I gesture into the darkness. 'The world at your feet.'

'Guess I'd rather be a big fish in a small pond than a nobody in an ocean.' She takes another swig. 'What brings *you* back here?'

'You heard about the medal?'

'Penny told me.'

'Errol's wife?'

She nods.

'You two talk?'

'She calls to update me sometimes. Errol and I can't be in the same room together, but I still like to know how he's getting on.'

I remembered how suspicious the girl had been. 'She was asking about me, wasn't she?'

'She just wanted to know what happened to your father. And how Errol was involved.'

'You told her?'

'What I knew.' She studies me over the rim of her glass. 'So, you came back here for old time's sake?'

'Not exactly. Did I ever talk to you about the night Dad died?'

She shakes her head. 'Only that Errol didn't do it.'

'Well, there was a sergeant with Dad on the island. His right-hand man, called Eugene.'

'And …?'

'When Eugene reported Dad missing, he said he'd waited at the jetty because Dad had ordered him to. He'd only started looking when it was pitch black and that was when the mob attacked him.'

'So?'

'After the ceremony Errol mentioned he'd seen Eugene with Dad right in the middle of the island … when it was still light.'

She shook her head. 'I don't understand.'

'It means he lied. Eugene lied.'

'And you think …?'

'I don't know what to think. Except there's something he didn't tell us, and I have to find out what it is.'

# Chapter 35

## Eugene

I roll onto my back and kick off the sheet. There's no air conditioner but the breeze through the louvres cools the sweat on my legs. A gecko darting across the ceiling feels like a good omen.

My head reminds me why I don't drink spirits, and the face in the bathroom mirror is a paler version of my usual self. It's better after I've splashed water on my face and pinched my cheeks but my hair's gone lank in the humidity so I tie it back like a schoolgirl. I select a simple shift, like I used to wear back then, and lip balm instead of lipstick.

It's eight o'clock and already I feel like I'm running late for an appointment.

Lucille is humming in the dining room. 'Take a seat and I'll bring over a coffee. You look like you could use it.'

'You're very chirpy.'

'All part of the job. So, you're off to find this policeman after breakfast?'

I nod.

'I can drive you to the police station.'

'Walking clears my head. If it's still safe to walk?'

'God yeah. It's not Moresby.' She places her hand on mine. 'I'm here if you need anything.'

I head out, with the strip of aquamarine between the sky and the shore as stunning as it always was, and the familiar crunch of ground coral beneath my feet.

The police station looks unchanged, except the pale-green paint is a little cracked. The dank smell remains. The young constable inside says he hasn't heard of Sergeant Eugene but explains he's new in town.

I stand outside the office, trying not to cry. I'd been so sure I'd find Eugene. I'd bumped straight into Lucille and I hadn't even been looking for her.

I glance at the track leading up to the police compound but there's no point; if Eugene's no longer a policeman, he won't be in the police compound. There used to be a little village just a bit further on though, near the point where Dad loved to fish, so I head in that direction.

The village is still there and it's grown to include shanties of blue tarpaulin as well as the traditional woven coconut fronds. Some kids are walking along the beach, trailing their legs through the shallows. Someone kicks up water and a splashing match erupts.

A couple of boats are pulled up on the beach past the village and a larger fishing boat is moored offshore. A wooden shed resembling an old-fashioned bathing box painted in red and blue stripes has been built since I was last here. A hand-painted sign hangs on the door. When I lean forward to read it, my heart jolts in my chest. *'Boats for hire. Proprietor: Eugene Tola.'*

It could be my Eugene. He spent a lot of time around boats and he was always fishing. I realise with a pang of shame that I don't know his surname.

There's a movement in the shadows under a coconut tree ahead. A figure's bent over a speedboat pulled up on the beach. As I approach, he straightens and tilts his head.

He's wearing a floppy terry-towelling hat like Dad used to and his skin's more weathered, but it's Eugene. As his face twists with emotion, my own tears take me by surprise.

'Miss Billie. What are you doing here?'

'I've been in Moresby. Errol gave Dad a medal. Remember Errol?'

He wipes his eyes, nods. 'I can't believe you here.'

'I came all this way to find you.'

It feels like a blessing meeting in this magic place, the waves lapping on the shore and the laughter of children tinkling on the breeze. I can't break the spell just yet.

'Do you take people out in your boat, Eugene?'

He nods.

'Then take me to Keriva.'

'What, now, miss?'

I check my watch. 'Plenty of time to get there and back today. Unless you've got another job?'

'No ...' The reluctance in his voice is matched by a resistance in his face.

I hold out a handful of kina notes but he shakes his head. 'No, missus. No money.'

'Please don't call me missus. Makes me feel like my mother.'

Finally, a smile. 'Okay ... Miss Billie. But me ham-mamus long helpim yu. You savvy?'

'You're happy to help?'

He nods but he looks anything but happy.

'Okay, let's go then. I'll just get one of these kids to run a note to Lucille at the club. Don't want her worrying about me, do we?'

I scribble a note telling Lucille that Eugene is taking me to Keriva and I should be back by dark, then give the oldest kid a kina to run it to the club.

I'm patting myself on the back as we wade through the warm shallows. Not only will Lucille know where and who I'm with, but Eugene knows she knows. We clamber on board the boat, anchored a long stone's throw from the beach. It has a small cabin to shade us from the sun but it's nowhere near as big as the trawler Dad used to take down to Keriva.

As we round the heads and travel southwards, the hull thumps against the waves. Eugene gives me a reassuring grin. 'No worry. I been down here plenty time. Plenty deep out there,' he points. 'Big fish.'

'And Keriva?'

He shakes his head as if I've suggested something improper. 'Never go back. Not in eleven year.'

'Eleven years? So, you quit the force after …'

'Me no quit.' A flash of resentment crosses his face and I remember his wife's anger that day in the compound. She had feared he would suffer because of my father's death, and it seems he had.

'I'm sorry.'

He shrugs.

As we head out into deeper water, I sneak a glance across. He stands steady at the wheel, comfortably in charge and just as dependable as he had been when he was a police-man. And yet he'd lied about that day.

I widen my stance to rise above the swell and as I find my sea legs my mind starts to pick over the loose threads. From Errol's revelation and the doubts it provoked about Eugene, through the whirlwind of Lucille and her vodka bottles, right up to the discovery of Eugene living my father's dream and wearing a hat so old and floppy it may well be one of his. The answer lies somewhere in this blur, if I can just focus.

My concentration is broken when Eugene calls out and points up to the white house looming over the channel.

'Is Masta Barry still there?'

'Emi die, maybe ten year?' Eugene pats his heart, grimacing.

'And the rest of the family?' I imagine Vanessa still watching from the lookout.

He shakes his head. 'Gone finish. Island co-op now. Your friend Errol fix that.'

'And how about your family? I remember your wife

and the little one that day I came to the compound.'

A smile splits his face. 'My Josephine in high school.'

'I can't believe that.'

The island suddenly emerges out of the water in vivid jungle green. Eugene throws the engine into neutral and jumps onto the jetty to tie us up. I recall the feeling of being out of my depth on this island.

Eugene extends his hand to help me off. I try to step across unaided but I misjudge the rise and fall of the boat and Eugene grabs my arm to steady me. I mumble thanks.

The trade store is still under the palms, wearing a fresh coat of orange paint. A sign proclaims it as a Keriva Co-operative Enterprise and a young girl sits inside, instead of Errol's mother.

I turn to Eugene. 'Where's May?'

'Errol build her big house in Kavieng.' Eugene is looking at me. 'What you want to do, miss?'

'I want to see … where it happencd. Where my father died.'

Eugene leads me off into the bush but he's dragging his feet like a kid on his first day of school. The cicadas are singing and the sun is blurring everything to white as we stumble towards the heart of the island. The path divides ahead and I recognise the turnoff to Tobias' spirit house.

We look at each other and move towards the spirit house in dread silence, although Tobias is long dead and his followers have surely faded away.

There's nothing in the clearing but some blackened stumps.

'Plenty fire,' Eugene whispers.

'So the malangans …'

'Emi die.' Eugene nods at the lumps of charcoal lying scattered around us on the sand. He shivers and it feels like we're standing in the ruin of a medieval cathedral.

'Who did this?'

He shakes his head. 'Me no savvy. Me stay long boat.'

The words I've been keeping for the right moment tumble out, 'But that's not true, is it Eugene?'

He's taken aback. 'What?'

'Errol said something the other day that didn't make sense to me. He said he couldn't understand why you never spoke up for him.'

'Spoke …?'

'He said you could have given him an alibi because you saw him leaving to go meet Vanessa. When you were with Dad in the middle of the island.'

There's a pause, long enough for me to hear distant waves under the buzzing of insects.

'You weren't waiting back at the boat, were you?' I read the guilt on his face. 'Why did you lie?'

He pulls a handkerchief from his pocket and holds it to his mouth like he's trying to stifle something.

When he finally speaks I can barely hear him. 'Me always 'fraid you ask me.'

'I never doubted you for a minute. Not one minute.'

'I tell you truth one time, Miss Billie. But you no listen.'

'What are you talking about?'

'I tell you mi bush kanaka tasol.'

'What did you mean by that?'

'Masta try teach me white man's law. If man break law, police take him calaboose. But malangan, spirit house … this *my* law. You understand?'

'Not really.'

'When Tobias show me malangan, it warning.'

'When what?'

'Remember, malangan in box outside haus bilong Tobias?'

He's talking about the figure in the cupboard with the cowrie eyes. 'How did you know it was a message for you? I saw it too.'

He shakes his head. 'It not your law.'

'He couldn't have known you'd find it.'

He looks at me like I'm stupid. 'Sangguma know all.'

'What do you mean by a warning, anyhow?'

'Bad things happen to man who go against malangan.'

'What did you do?'

His voice drops. 'When young fella leave, Tobias send me kisim knife, bringim back …' He reads the judgement on my face. 'I swear, miss, me think emi humbug, make Masta think boy no good.'

'But …'

'When I get back, Masta not here. Tobias run way and me lukim … blood.'

'Blood?'

'Masta, emi lie long ground … emi die pinis.'

'So, you went back to the boat, went up to the house, raised the alarm, stood by while Errol got arrested, watched my family destroyed – and all the time you *knew* Tobias killed my father?' The anger feels like it's going to explode out of my chest.

But Eugene's not listening to me. At first I think he's just avoiding my eyes, but then I realise he's staring at a spot beside us. His focus is intense and his eyes full of dread. I follow his gaze.

One of the *malangans* has escaped the fires. It's standing on the edge of the clearing facing us. The paint on its face is a ghostly white and the cowrie eyes have rolled back in its head so they seem to be looking up at us. Eugene's eyes are bulging and he doesn't seem to hear me call his name. I grab his arm to try and get his attention but he's rooted to the spot and much too strong to budge.

Just then something yellow deeper in the bush catches my eye. It's a plastic flag, the kind our Phys Ed teacher used to mark javelin throws, beside a log a few yards into the undergrowth. There's a dark patch on the ground next to it. Logic tells me it can't possibly be Dad's blood after all these years, but I bash forward until I'm staring down at it.

Something like a cry pierces the air. It sounded like it was coming from behind me, so I scramble back to the clearing. And that's when I see Eugene flat on his back, staring up at the sky.

# Chapter 36

## Pedro

I try shaking Eugene but his eyes are glazed. He doesn't seem to be breathing so I move his head back to open his airway. I can't find a pulse so I put my hands on his chest and start pushing down hard and fast. When I take a rest, I shout for help. I don't think anyone will hear me, but I don't know what else to do. I wonder if I should run to the village but I can't leave him alone in this place.

He remains still.

'Please wake up,' I whisper.

Then a whistle shrills. I scream for help again and a policeman appears. He drops to his knees on the other side of Eugene and continues CPR. I watch in awe as he works, so much calmer and more efficiently than I was. After what feels like forever, he stands and shakes his head.

'No, he can't be dead. He can't be …'

There's a gentle pressure on my elbow as the policeman tries to lift me, but I slide out of his grip and lurch forward, desperate to deliver my message. 'It's okay, I understand. You weren't to blame.'

Eugene's face remains a mask.

The policeman offers his hand again. 'What's your name?'

'Billie. Billie Cleary. Sorry, who are you?'

'Sergeant Hari. I'm in charge of Conos Station.'

I think back to Vanessa's party and the police who had come from Conos to investigate the finger in the mail.

'How come you're here?'

'Your friend from The Kavieng Club got on to head-quarters about trouble out here.'

Thank goodness for Lucille.

'I appreciate you coming all this way, I really do.'

He shrugs it off. 'Couldn't do much, I'm afraid. Was he a friend of yours?'

I nod. 'He was a policeman too, a long time ago. My father was a kiap, they worked together.'

He frowns. 'A kiap was killed out here a while back.'

'Yes, that was …'

'I'm sorry, I didn't realise.'

'How could you?'

He's studying me. 'You mentioned blame just now?'

'The sergeant blamed himself for not stopping my father's death.'

'And you came here together …?'

'I asked him to show me … where it happened.'

'That must have been a very difficult experience.'

There's a long silence. His words echo in my mind and I suddenly realise what he's getting at. I've brought a reluctant man to a place of extreme stress and it appears that man has died of a heart attack. I'm somehow implicated in his death, even if I hadn't intended it. His wife and the daughter in high school are going to be without the family breadwinner because of me.

Sergeant Hari coughs. 'I've got to escort the body back, but I'll take you over to the co-op and see if anyone can give you a lift to Kavieng.'

The trip across the strait is a blur. In no time at all we're standing in front of the copra shed. The dark interior feels empty without Don's booming presence.

A young islander sitting at the desk looks up. 'Afternoon,

Hari.' He stands and shakes the sergeant's hand. 'We didn't call you, did we?'

'No,' the sergeant says. 'Miss Cleary here chartered a boat to Keriva and the driver's had a heart attack. Fatal, I'm afraid.'

'That's too bad.' The young man smiles at me. 'So, you're stranded?'

I nod.

'I was hoping you could spare one of your fellows to run her up to Kavieng?'

'Of course. I'll take her myself. I was going up in the morning anyway. Just give me a minute?'

'Sure.' The sergeant holds the door open and we move outside.

'I better get back,' Hari says. 'You're in good hands, anyway.'

'What will happen to Eugene?'

'He'll be taken to Kavieng for an autopsy. You better go to the police station when you arrive back, they'll want a statement.'

The young man emerges from the shed. 'I'm Pedro, by the way.' He leads me to a Land Cruiser.

There's a long silence as we start the drive with only the whoosh of the tyres ringing in my ears. Just when I think that's how it's going to be, he speaks. 'The driver died then?'

I nod, not trusting my voice to hold up.

'That must have been a shock. I don't mean to be rude but you look familiar. I don't s'pose you've been here before?'

There's something familiar about him too. Then it hits me. He was one of the boys who followed us that first day Dad took me to the island. The one out in front.

'You were one of Errol's boys, weren't you?'

He grins. 'He used to call me his little foreman.'

'My dad was the DC. I came quite a few times before … before he died.'

'That was a terrible thing.'

'You were there that night?'

'I was on the island but I didn't see anything.'

'What happened to Tobias' spirit house?'

'It got burnt.'

'Who burnt it?'

'*We* did. That little weasel didn't come forward when Errol was arrested and people were still afraid to speak against his magic. We had to show that the malangans were just lumps of wood. So, we burnt the whole lot to the ground. And guess what? Nothing happened.'

'But Errol believed in magic. He told me.'

'He knew the magic had to be faced if we wanted to defeat Tobias.'

I think back to the afternoon Dad had laughed off Errol's warning about the old man. Things might have been different if he'd listened. It had been my schoolgirl infatuation with Errol that had made Dad so hostile.

'So, Errol put you in charge as a reward for backing him?'

He shakes his head. 'I'm not in charge, it's a co-op.'

'And the co-op was Errol's idea?'

He nods. 'He got it for a good price after the fat masta died. But he bought it for the island.'

'How do you mean, for the island?'

'*He* paid the money but we all own it. You remember those young boys who used to sit around under the trees doing nothing? Errol's given them a job. He's done so much more for us than his lousy uncle.'

'Cedric?'

Pedro nods. 'That greedy bastard's a politician. Errol's a leader. You understand the difference?'

'Aren't you worried the Moresby dirt will rub off on him?'

He looks confused. 'Rub off?'

'Aren't you worried he'll get corrupted by all that money flying around?'

He takes his eyes off the road to give me a hard look. 'You saw him – what do you think?'

I laugh nervously. 'I'm not sure.'

'Well, *I* am sure,' he says firmly. 'He'll *never* be like Cedric.'

He fixes his eyes on the road, and I think about how I'm going to face the tattooed woman and her child.

# Chapter 37

## Reunion

Pedro pulls up outside the Kavieng police station. 'Do you want me to come in with you?'

I nod. His kindness has brought a lump to my throat.

The first person I see inside is Eugene's wife. She's sitting in an office behind the counter, just visible through an open door. Something in the fall of her head suggests she's heard the bad news.

An older policeman emerges from the office and walks towards me. 'Miss Cleary?' He faces me across the counter. 'Mr Chan told me you'd be coming.'

'Errol?' I stammer. 'But how …?'

'I called him,' Pedro says. 'I knew he'd want to know.'

Over the policeman's shoulder, I can see the woman

staring at me through the gap in the door. Her look is an accusation I can't face; I focus instead on the policeman. 'You've told Eugene's wife?'

The policeman nods. 'Hari asked me to tell her and the girl.'

'His child's here too?'

'Yep.'

'Can I talk to them?'

He hesitates. 'Let's just get your statement down.'

The sun's going down as Pedro pulls into the club carpark. It's hard to believe it was only this morning I set out in search of Eugene so full of optimism. It feels like a lifetime ago.

Pedro opens my door. 'Lucille will look after you.'

'You've been very kind, thank you.'

I step down and hold out my hand. He takes it for the briefest moment.

With a flash of taillights, the Land Cruiser disappears through the gates, leaving me feeling totally alone.

As I approach the bar, familiar voices rise above the hubbub and Rosie and Susan appear like a mirage, sitting on two bar stools.

'What are you two doing here?'

'Aren't you pleased to see us?' Rosie says.

I burst into tears. The two of them rush forward and we rock together in a clumsy embrace.

Lucille puts two cocktails down on the counter and pats the empty bar stool. 'Sit down, Billie, while I make you one of these.'

'We're here because of your friend Errol,' Susan says. 'He came out to the airport to say goodbye and he was shocked when we told him you'd come here alone. We talked for ages until he convinced us to come too. By that stage we'd missed the plane home *and* the plane up here, so he put us up in a fancy airport hotel.'

'He didn't come with you?'

'Said he didn't want to intrude.'

'How did you find me?'

'Lucille picked us up from the airport.'

'I didn't think you guys even knew each other.'

'Errol lined that up too.'

Lucille puts the gaudy blue cocktail in front of me. 'You've had a rough day, kiddo.'

'I haven't even thanked you for calling the police, Lucille. Hari may not have been able to save Eugene but he sure as hell helped me.'

She gave a gracious shrug.

'How did you know?'

'Just had a bad feeling.'

'So, you were there … when it happened?' Rosie winces.

'I *made* him go there. He didn't want to, but I had to see the actual spot …'

Her voice is soothing. 'You couldn't have known what would happen.'

It's tempting to keep Eugene's confession secret and accept my sisters' reassurances. But there have been too many secrets already.

I take a deep breath. 'I should have picked up on his fear. He was terrified I'd find out.'

'Find out what?'

'Tobias made him fetch Errol's knife from his hut. He thought it was to discredit Errol, he didn't realise it was a trick to leave Dad unprotected. Until he got back and found his body …'

'So, are you saying …?'

'Tobias made him an accomplice. He's carried that guilt ever since.'

'Maybe part of him wanted to confess,' Susan says.

I take a sip of the sweet, fiery cocktail. 'But I didn't get a chance to tell him I understood … he never meant Dad to die.'

'It must be a relief to know Errol wasn't involved,' Rosie says.

'Dad went out there to warn Errol off Vanessa.'

'Vanessa *Barry*?' Susan sounds sceptical.

I look at Rosie. '*You're* not surprised, are you?'

She pulls a face. 'Vanessa wasn't as posh as she made out.'

'Errol didn't like Dad treating him like a naughty schoolboy, so when he saw him going into the bush with Tobias, he said nothing, although he knew it looked wrong. If they hadn't had that argument about me ...'

'Give yourself a break, kiddo.' Lucille pats my hand. 'You loved your father and you loved Eugene and you've lost them both. Stop blaming yourself.'

# Chapter 38

## Josephine

I wake early after a fitful sleep, an urgency in my belly like I've got an important exam.

The coral dawn is spreading across the sky and there's activity out on the street. Women with loaded *bilums* and trailing children are heading for the market at the bottom of the hill. It's comforting to have company.

They turn left and I turn right and head past the village. When I get to Eugene's boathouse the door is locked, so I keep walking along the beach towards Dad's special fishing spot. It's only when I'm almost at the bend that I spy the house nestled under the spreading fig tree. Its door is the same brilliant blue as the boathouse, and I know immediately this is where Eugene's widow lives.

The front door opens and a teenaged girl stands tall in the doorway. This must be Josephine, the daughter Eugene was so proud of. She's wearing a school dress and I recognise the crest of Utu High School, where Dad used to show those Clark Gable films. Her mother follows her and leans over to stroke her daughter's hair before the girl strides off down the road.

The woman wipes a tear from her eye as she watches the girl disappear and I realise it would be wrong to intrude. I turn and begin walking back towards the market when I see a group of students milling around Josephine. They're all in the Utu uniform and just then a minibus pulls up alongside and they clamber aboard.

A crackling megaphone interrupts my thoughts, coming from the direction of the market. A woman is shouting rhythmically in Pidgin, and as I get closer, I realise she's preaching.

'Richpela papa i sing out, "Piccaninny bilong mi emi kam back." Emi word bilong God.'

It's the parable of the prodigal son; he who was lost now is found, and there's more rejoicing over one lost soul than countless good ones.

The woman's voice becomes a soundtrack beneath the chatter of locals bartering and filling their *bilums* with bananas, coconuts and vegetables. There's a warm feeling to the bustle as I wander up and down the rows of stallholders.

'Miss Billie?'

Suriwan is standing in front of me with a full basket and a face-splitting smile. She pulls me into a bear hug and I close my eyes as I breathe in her familiar smell.

'You're still here. I thought you would have gone back to the Highlands, you know, after independence.'

She shakes her head. 'So many wantoks buried here. Even Tahl.'

'Oh no. I'm sorry.'

She winces and we stand in silence for a moment.

'And your children?'

She brightens. 'My eldest is a nurse like Miss Susan. And my boy is in Rabaul on a scholarship.'

'That's brilliant.'

'You come back, Miss Billie?'

'Only for a few days. Hey, Rosie and Susan are here too. They'd love to see you.'

She looks at her basket. 'Me housekeeper now.'

'A housekeeper? That's great. Who do you work for?'

'Nice lady, name Miss May.'

'I think I know her. Is her son a member of parliament?'

She nods. 'He give me job.'

'I'd love to catch up with May. Could I come home with

you, maybe ask her to the club for lunch?'

Suriwan hesitates. 'She shy. Maybe me ask?'

'I'd love that. Come down to the club – my sisters would love to see you.'

When I arrive back at the club, I find Lucille in the kitchen with some trussed crabs.

'Hi, kiddo. You missed breakfast.'

'It's okay, I got some mango cheeks at the market.'

'You got up early to go to the market?'

'I was going to see Eugene's widow.'

'That would have been awkward.'

'Actually, I decided not to go. It didn't feel right, intruding on them.'

'Very wise.'

'Can I ask you a favour?'

'Name it.'

'I need to call Desmond. I'll pay, of course.'

'It would be my pleasure. International calls don't always work though.'

The big red telephone is sitting on top of a South Pacific towel on the bar. Lucille dials a few numbers and then hands the base to me. 'It's ready for the area code and your number. Good luck.'

As I'm listening to the ringing buzz, I realise Desmond will most likely be out on a job. Then there's a click and he answers, 'Hello.'

'It's me.'

'Billie. It's so good to hear your voice.' His voice catches.

'I want to come home.'

'Are you okay?'

'I'm okay but I need you.'

'I miss you so much it hurts.'

I close my eyes and picture the smile that makes me melt.

'I'll drive up and get you from Brisbane,' he says.

I'm not sure how long it'll take. I'll call you again from Moresby.'

'I love you.'

'Not as much as I love you.'

# Chapter 39

## Full circle

I can hear Rosie shrieking as I hang up the phone. Suriwan and my sisters are hugging and dancing around at the top of the front steps.

Suriwan's eyes gleam. 'Miss May ask you for lunch.'

Turns out Errol built May a house next to our old one, so we stop for a look. There's a Statesman in the driveway; we're not sure if it's the one Julius drove or not but its mirrors are draped with cobwebs. The house looks similarly neglected. The paintwork is peeling and weeds sprout between the hibiscus bushes.

'I thought this was the Provincial Governor's now?' Susan says.

'It looks a bit sad, doesn't it,' Rosie says.

'I guess the money's just not there for this kind of thing.'

I remember we used prisoners to tend our gardens. 'The calaboose used to do it but that's probably not allowed anymore.'

The front entrance to May's house is more like how I remember our old house. White coral crunches under our feet and pink hibiscus bushes look well-tended.

Suriwan leads us to the dining table set with white china and crystal, a bottle of champagne ready in an ice bucket.

May glides in. Her halo of hair has turned white but her skin still glows.

I step forward. 'I'm not sure if you remember me?'

'Of course I do, Billie.' Her voice and her smile are stronger than I was expecting.

'It's very kind of you to have us.'

Suriwan pops the cork.

'What are we celebrating?' Susan asks.

'Being back with old friends, silly,' Rosie says.

'My boy's very keen you enjoy your stay,' May says.

'Oh, we are,' we chorus.

'He's a good boy,' she says.

The comment hangs in the air.

There's a distant rap and Suriwan heads towards the front door.

I nod towards her disappearing form. 'It was good of Errol to offer her a job.'

May smiles. 'I don't know where I'd be without her now.'

A male voice echoes down the hall and Pedro appears behind Suriwan. 'I'm sorry to interrupt, but I've got something to show you, Billie.'

He passes me an object wrapped in a small *lap-lap*. It's a *malangan*, glaring up at me with a set of white teeth and a fierce expression.

'You know what this is?'

'A malangan?'

'Not just any malangan.'

I look at the cowrie eyes rolling back in the head and I can hear the buzz of the insects in the clearing.

'It was on the island. When Eugene ...'

He nods. 'They brought it up as evidence.'

I wrap the *lap-lap* around it and pass it back to him. 'What are you going to do with it?'

'I'm taking it back there to burn in the clearing. And this time I'll make sure *he* is finished off.'

'He?'

'Don't you recognise him?'

I'm reluctant to say the word. 'Tobias?'

He nods. 'That's why I brought him to you. So

you understand your father will have his payback. And Eugene too.'

'Why don't you girls go outside and I'll bring some tea,' says May.

We farewell Pedro and head out to a wide verandah very similar to ours, except the cane furniture looks brand new. The jungle fringe on the edge of the garden has been cut back to give a panoramic view of the harbour.

Suriwan brings a platter of tropical fruit.

'One of Suriwan's daughters is a nurse,' I say. 'I think you inspired her, Susan.'

'I'm honoured.'

Suriwan beams.

'And your son has a scholarship?' I ask.

'To school in Rabaul.'

A scholarship … I remember the throng waiting near the market to clamber onto the minibus. 'So, Utu doesn't have a scholarship?'

Suriwan shakes her head.

I turn to my sisters. 'I think I've just thought of a perfect legacy. A scholarship in Dad's name to the local high school. You remember Utu?'

'That's a great idea.' Rosie beams.

'I'm sure Errol would help us, he knows how these things work,' Susan says.

'And we know the perfect candidate to be the first recipient,' I add.

The three of us smile at each other as May comes out with the tea.

For the first time I actually look at the view. 'Wow, you can see straight across to Nusa.'

Susan looks at me. 'We should go there before we leave.'

'Of course, we should.'

'It *is* a lovely little island,' May says.

'It's not just that. It's where we scattered … my father's ashes. I can't believe I didn't think of it until now.'

'There's still time,' May says. 'Lucille very good at arranging things.'

My sisters and I grip our seats as spray flies up in our faces. Two of Lucille's staff are taking us over to the twin islands in a speedboat. Dusk is deepening to indigo, just as it did the last time we were here. As we approach, a campfire is visible beside the channel. It looks like a village has sprung up in the very spot where we used to picnic.

'You want get down?' The helmsman nods towards the shore.

'We don't need to intrude. Can you just make the motor quiet for a moment?'

The engine drops to a purr so we can hear the waves lapping against the hull. My sisters and I reach for each other's hands. The hull rocks and we look down into the black sea. I run my free hand through the water. It's blood warm. 'Dad feels close here, doesn't he?'

Rosie nods. 'It was worth coming all this way just for this moment.'

'I was so afraid to come back, you know.'

'Why?' Rosie asks.

'I thought I might hate it. Or love it so much I never wanted to leave again. Neither of which are true.'

'I know what you mean,' Susan says. 'It's nice to visit …'

'But it's not home anymore, is it?'

My thoughts jump ahead to the coming day. The three of us haven't spent so much time together since, well, that last Christmas up here; it's going to be hard to part with my sisters at Brisbane Airport. 'I'm going to miss you two.'

'We better make sure we catch up more often then,' Susan says.

We sit listening as an undercurrent of voices and a distant guitar carry across from the village on the evening breeze.

Finally, Susan looks to me. 'Did you find what you were looking for?'

Images of the last few days scroll through my mind. Errol's candlelit confession, the poignancy of Dad's ceremony and the elation of the ten-year independence celebration, my emotion at finding Eugene followed by the shock of his guilty revelation and death. Wading through the aftermath like wet cement until I saw Josephine and her schoolmates and realised how we could make some sense of it all.

'Actually, it does feel like something has fallen into place. Like Dad can rest in peace. And so can I.'

'Goodbye, Daddy,' Rosie whispers.

I turn to the helmsman. 'We're ready to go back now.'

# Acknowledgements

Personal experience, folklore and anecdotes were supplemented by the following invaluable sources, whom I thank and acknowledge:

Hank Nelson's excellent *Taim bilong masta: the Australian involvement with Papua New Guinea*, especially for the chapter title 'Going Finish', which covered Independence, the exodus of Australian expats and 'the force [PNG] exerts over thousands of Australian memories.'

James Sinclair's *Kiap: Australia's patrol officers in Papua New Guinea*, especially on cargo cults.

*Pidgin English: grammar and dictionary of Neo-Melanesian* by Rev. Francis Mihalic.

*Cousteau's Papua New Guinea Journey* by Jean-Michel Cousteau and Mose Richards, especially on shark hunting in New Ireland.

Lonely Planet's *Papua New Guinea: a travel survival guide*, especially on Malangan carvings.

Finally, I'd like to thank everyone who's encouraged me along the way, including the VPLA, my CAE writing group, family, and my editor Claire McGregor and cover designer Hamish Payne.

# About the author

Mandy Maroney only lived in Papua New Guinea for her first sixteen years but the country left an indelible mark. She has always loved books and writing. An earlier version of *Going finish* won the Victorian Premier's Literary Award for an Unpublished Manuscript in 2008, and after many rewrites she is finally launching it into the world. She lives by the sea in Melbourne with partner Michael, a dog and two cats.

Connect with Mandy at:

Instagram: https://www.instagram.com/mandym592/

Facebook: mandy.maroney.2025